He glared up at her as she approached. "I got mean friends with a long reach." His voice came out a breathy snarl. "You won't keep hold of me. They'll kill you."

Ignoring the threats, Bree leaned toward the fugitive. "Leon Deering, I'm arresting you on suspicion of—"

A rifle blast echoed through the canyon. Bree began to whirl toward the rancher who must have shot at her.

Then a heavy body slammed into her, thrusting her toward a crevice in the rock face, and time snapped back into sync. Bree fought, kicking and attempting to headbutt her traitorous neighbor. Her rifle was out of play, crushed between their struggling bodies. Together, they struck the unforgiving stone wall, and the shade of the crevice enveloped them.

"Stop fighting." Cameron's voice snarled in her ear. "It wasn't me. Someone's shooting from above."

Bree went still. Pregnant silence fell. Bree's heart hammered in her chest.

Then another sharp report quickly followed by a third sent shards of rock ricocheting into their meager hideout.

Jill Elizabeth Nelson writes what she likes to read—faith-based tales of adventure seasoned with romance. Parts of the year find her and her husband on the international mission field. Other parts find them at home in rural Minnesota, surrounded by the woods and prairie and their four grown children and young grandchildren. More about Jill and her books can be found at jillelizabethnelson.com or Facebook.com/jillelizabethnelson.author.

Books by Jill Elizabeth Nelson

Love Inspired Suspense

Evidence of Murder
Witness to Murder
Calculated Revenge
Legacy of Lies
Betrayal on the Border
Frame-Up
Shake Down
Rocky Mountain Sabotage
Duty to Defend
Lone Survivor
The Baby's Defender
Hunted for Christmas
In Need of Protection
Unsolved Abduction
Hunted in Alaska
Safeguarding the Baby
Targeted for Elimination
Texas Revenge Target

Visit the Author Profile page at LoveInspired.com.

Texas Revenge Target

JILL ELIZABETH NELSON

LOVE INSPIRED SUSPENSE

INSPIRATIONAL ROMANCE

LOVE INSPIRED® SUSPENSE
INSPIRATIONAL ROMANCE

ISBN-13: 978-1-335-63829-8

Texas Revenge Target

Copyright © 2024 by Jill Elizabeth Nelson

Recycling programs for this product may not exist in your area.

Love Inspired
22 Adelaide St. West, 41st Floor
Toronto, Ontario M5H 4E3, Canada
www.LoveInspired.com

Printed in Lithuania

MIX
Paper | Supporting responsible forestry
FSC® C021394

From the end of the earth will I cry unto thee,
when my heart is overwhelmed:
lead me to the rock that is higher than I.
—*Psalm* 61:2

To those who bravely battle forces attacking their lives (addiction, illness, relationship problems, financial woes, ad infinutum), who daily lean on the Everlasting Rock.

ONE

Texas Ranger Brianna Maguire—Bree, if a person wanted to stay on her good side—leaned back in the saddle as she guided her palomino gelding, Teton, down the semisteep grade of a dry wash. Her stomach roiled, but not because she doubted Teton's surefootedness. Images of the too recent shootout between law enforcement and a violent gang of cattle rustlers kept intruding on her concentration and freezing the breath in her lungs.

Had that life-altering event happened a mere thirty-six hours ago? An eternity had passed and yet only a moment since she'd shot a crook, but not in time to prevent her Special Response Team colleague, Will Stout, from taking a fatal bullet. If only she'd been a split second faster, Will might be alive, and his two young children might still have a daddy. But it was the rustler who had survived, though he'd likely spend the rest of his life behind bars and in a wheelchair. If any satisfaction existed in that knowledge, it tasted bitter.

Chipped rock and pebbles disturbed by Teton's big hooves skittered ahead of them into the ravine's mesquite-tufted floor. Saddle leather creaked, the gelding snorted, and Bree began a soft, encouraging patter with her voice. Odors of desert plants and dust teased her nostrils, and she swallowed a sneeze as Teton brought her to the bottom of the gash carved in the terrain by flash floods over time immemorial. Her pulse rate spiked at another splotch of red glistening on a rock. She followed the telltale mark to the right, deeper into this fold in the tableland.

The midmorning sun beat down on Bree's shoulders and she swiped the arm of her long-sleeved shirt across her forehead beneath the brim of her Stetson hat. Late summer's intense heat baked West Texas's arid Llano Estacado prairie, and she couldn't allow sweat to dim her vision. If the sporadic blood droplets she was following came from a human being, she could be on the trail of Leon Waring, the fugitive leader of the cattle rustlers.

In the violent shootout between a joint law enforcement task force and his rustler gang near the town of Levelland, Waring had been wounded. The gun battle had left several dead, including Will, as well as numerous injured, on both sides. Of the criminal gang, Waring and one or two low-level desperados had escaped. A statewide manhunt was underway for Waring, in particular—a manhunt that she was no longer officially a part of due to being placed on leave after shooting someone in the line of duty. Leave was standard procedure, and Bree had no doubt the review of her actions would shortly result in restoration to active service, but she had no intention of sitting out the hunt for Waring.

She was the only one who seemed to think the fugitive, escaping cross-country into the night on an ATV, had headed into the Llano to hide. Everyone else was looking east, where larger towns and cities would afford medical care and a place to hide for a wounded crook. But Waring was born and bred on the Llano, and if his wound wasn't too bad, this was where he'd go. And Bree was just the person to hunt him down. The Llano was her childhood backyard, too.

So, like any other sensible veteran of law enforcement, she'd taken advantage of the unexpected leave to go home. But when she'd reached the familiar comfort of the Double-Bar-M, the ranch she co-owned with her brother, she'd saddled up Teton and headed out. Apprehending Waring was a personal mission, even though finding a trace of him in the vast rugged country wasn't likely. She simply needed to feel like she was doing something productive.

Bree had not located the crook's ATV or even ATV tracks, but then the sudden appearance of blood droplets had given her renewed but guarded hope. The blood trail could well come from an animal, and one of God's creatures might need to be mercifully put down. If so, she'd have to deal with the frustration of not locating the violent crook. Too bad the terrain made sneaking up on whatever lay ahead nearly impossible.

Her horse's shod hooves clicked sporadically against scattered stones. As the wash deepened into a canyon strewn with boulders and dark crevices, Bree kept her head on a swivel and her ears perked for any indication of an ambush. Sounds foreign to the natural environment reached her ears and Bree tugged Teton to a halt. The animal stood still, head high, ears aimed forward toward a bend in the canyon. Clearly, the gelding heard the murmur, too.

Human voices?

Bree swung her leg off the saddle and lowered herself to stand beside her horse. She dropped the ends of the reins to the earth. Teton was trained to remain in place when his reins were grounded by his rider. With one hand, Bree pulled her rifle from the saddle holster and unsnapped the sidearm at her belt with the other. She might be happening upon an innocent situation, like cowhands out looking for strays, but she wasn't about to discount potential danger. Not with a desperate criminal at large and the blood trail that had led her here.

Carefully placing her booted feet to avoid loose rocks or brittle vegetation, Bree made her way toward the bend in the canyon. When she reached the curve, she halted and squatted behind a boulder. Slowly, she peered out from behind cover and bottled a gasp.

She'd been right to believe the notorious rustler had fled to the Llano. His burly form leaned up against the cliff wall. A bloody arm hung limply at his side, but the other arm pointed a pistol at a man who stood with his back to her but trained a rifle in the rustler's direction. Apparently, Bree had been mistaken that she was the only one pursuing Waring into the wilderness. Then again, this could be a random encounter between the fugitive and a local hand. The guy was dressed like a rancher in faded and dusty denim pants, a long-sleeved checked shirt, and a sweat-stained cowboy hat. However, with only the broad back of the rifleman to go on, she couldn't claim to recognize the person engaged in the standoff with the wounded rustler.

"I'm more willing to shoot than you are," Waring snarled, a manic glint in his inky eyes. The sheen of sweat coating his scruffy face glistened in the sun. "I'll blast you before you pull the trigger. Now, drop that weapon and get out of here before I put you down."

Bree opened her mouth to warn the guy not to believe Waring would allow him to leave.

"This rifle's got a hair trigger." The man's words emerged, steady as the rock she hid behind. "If you shoot me, it'll go off, and we'll both be buzzard food."

Bree didn't recognize the deep voice. Who *was* this stranger and how had he ended up confidently facing off with a fugitive?

"Now, put your gun down," the man went on, "and I'll do the same. Then I'll treat your wound. You're not looking so well, buddy."

The crook's face crinkled in a snarl and his body tensed, preparing for action.

"Drop it, Waring!" Bree stood tall and stepped forward, rifle at the ready. "If this guy doesn't shoot you, I will."

The fugitive's fevered gaze swiveled toward her, along with the barrel of his gun. As the direction of the rustler's weapon shifted, the rifle in the stranger's grip blasted. Waring's pistol flew from his hand. The crook doubled over and sank to the ground, clutching both arms to his chest. Even if the stranger's bullet had struck only Waring's gun, the impact would have hurt—maybe even broken a bone in the fugitive's gun hand.

The stranger turned his head to Bree and his smoke-gray eyes met her green ones. Nope, this guy was not among her law enforcement colleagues, nor was he a local rancher. She knew all the owners and ranch hands in this area. If she'd ever met this man before, she would have remembered him—not only for his rugged good looks, but from the faint but distinctive scar that arched a one-sided parenthesis from the corner of his left eye almost to his ear and then nearly to the edge of his firm mouth. Whoever he was, the squint lines around his eyes labeled him a long-time outdoorsman, and the traces of silver at the temples of his short sable-brown hair suggested an age only slightly greater than her own forty-three years.

Now, for the big question—was he friend or foe? The guy had shot the weapon out of Leon Waring's hand, swift and accurate as a striking rattler.

Bree kept her rifle at the ready. "Texas Ranger Bree Maguire. And you are?"

Tension drained from the stranger's face and he lowered his weapon. "Cameron Wolfe. You must be Dillon Maguire's sister. He's told me about you." The edges of the man's lips tilted upward in a slight smile.

Bree's gut clenched. Why would this guy know Dillon and what had been said?

The man's smile turned to a grin. "Relax. I'm your new neighbor. I bought the Franklin place."

Bree huffed. She'd known the Franklin heirs were selling out after the death of their father because none of them had any interest in ranching, but Dillon had failed to tell her the place had sold. However, to be fair, she had pretty much blown onto the ranch site and blown right out again on Teton without saying much more than *Hi* and *Be back later* to her brother. Dillon would have tried to talk her out of traipsing the Llano on her own, but the bloody shootout near Levelland had disturbed her on levels she hadn't come to terms with yet, and she'd needed to be alone. Finding Waring's trail was a happy result that she now had to conclude properly.

"Pleased to meet you, neighbor, but I have to secure this prisoner." Reaching for the zip ties she kept in a pouch on her belt, Bree lowered her rifle and stepped past Cameron's tall, sturdy figure. "This man is a wanted cattle rustler and murderer."

A crumpled, bleeding mess, Waring glared up at her as she approached. "I got mean friends with a long reach." His voice came out a breathy snarl. "You won't keep hold of me. They'll kill you."

Ignoring the threats, Bree leaned toward the fugitive. "Leon Waring, I'm arresting you on suspicion of—"

A sharp tug on the ponytail that hung down her back coincided with a rifle blast echoing through the canyon. In her peripheral vision, strands of flame-red hair floated free of her head as time seemed to slow to a crawl. The fugitive's eyes went wide, fixed on her. The rifle in Bree's hand suddenly weighed a ton, dragging against her arms as she forced it up to her shoulder. She began to whirl on the rancher, who must have shot at her, every movement constrained as if by quicksand.

Then a heavy body slammed into her, thrusting her into a crevice in the rock face, and time snapped back into sync. Bree fought, kicking and attempting to head-butt her traitorous neighbor. Her rifle was out of play, crushed between their struggling bodies. Together, they struck the unforgiving stone wall and the shade of the crevice enveloped them.

"Stop fighting," Cameron's voice rasped in her ear. "It wasn't me. Someone's shooting from above."

Bree went still, the sense of his words penetrating her fierce resistance. Every detail of her surroundings etched upon her consciousness—the throbbing of her pulse in her ears, the groaning of the wounded crook on the other side of the crevice, the chill of the rock at her back, and the lingering odor of gun smoke overlaid by the buttery-leather aftershave her neighbor wore.

Pregnant silence fell. Bree's heart hammered in her chest.

Then another sharp report quickly followed by a third sent shards of rock ricocheting into their meager hide. Most peppered the stone face around them, but one stung Bree's cheek, sending a warm trickle down her face. By her neighbor's sudden grunt, one or more bits of shrapnel must have hit him also.

At best, the sniper above could hold them in the crevice until his ammo ran out. Then they could break cover and go after him. At worst, if this was one of Waring's alleged friends, the fugitive could overcome his wounds and recover his gun. Then she and her new neighbor would be at the ruthless criminal's mercy.

Cam breathed in the earthy scent of horse mixed with a pleasant fresh-rain shampoo the woman used. Her height—approximately five and a half feet if he had to estimate—put the top of her head just under his nose. The crevice in the canyon wall was not nearly big enough for two adults, even if one of them was a slender female. If the gunman above got the right angle for his shot, he could bounce a bullet off the rock right into one of them. Then there was the wounded desperado the redheaded ranger had attempted to arrest. He might recover enough to attack them as well. They couldn't stay where they were in the hope of survival, yet he had no safe exit strategies in mind.

But when had "safe" ever been a part of his life?

"I'm going to duck and roll toward that boulder a few feet from us. Cover me while I do that. From there, I may be able to spot the shooter and put him out of commission."

"Right." Bree jerked a nod. "I'll keep the attacker busy dodging bullets."

Cam grinned, meeting the ranger's steady gaze. She was no-nonsense. No argument. The ranger knew what needed to be done and was ready to do it—an attitude he immensely appreciated. People who ran rather than stood had once cost him everything worthwhile in his life—except faith in God, and sometimes he barely clung to that. Firming his jaw, he batted away the swarming memories and stuffed the pain back down into the black hole where it belonged. Now was not the time to wallow. If ever he permitted that time to come.

With no further thought or discussion, Cam dropped and rolled out of cover. A bullet slapped the rock face above him, but a cacophony of fire from Bree halted the attack. Since she couldn't see the assailant, she might not be sending bullets anywhere near him, but only an idiot would put his head up under that firestorm.

Cam reached the boulder and crouched behind it. He readied his rifle and ventured a peek past the cover of the rock toward the cliff top about fifteen feet up. The ranger's firing ceased and silence rang as loudly as gunfire.

Then the top of a Western hat peeked above the cliff's edge. Cam fired, and the hat flew. A loud yelp carried from above. He'd either hit the sniper or scared him silly. A receding scramble of feet on loose scree met his ears. Had the shooter fled?

Cam turned his head toward Bree, still undercover in the crevice. She met his gaze with wide eyes and a shrug of her shoulders. The shadow of her hideaway softened the clear-cut planes of her face, lending an exotic flavor to her striking features. Bree Maguire was not pretty—that description was entirely too bland. Nor was she beautiful in the standard sense. Yet a guy would look twice when she passed by. For sure and certain. Cam tore his gaze away and concentrated on listening.

No sound came from the wounded man Bree had addressed as Leon Waring. Had the man fled? Or had he retrieved his gun and now awaited someone brave or dumb enough to poke their head out? Must be his day for being brave or dumb because he ventured a peek. Then he drew back, processing what he had seen.

He settled grim eyes on Bree. "I don't think you're going to have to arrest that Waring fellow."

"He escaped?" Her tone held equal parts anger and anguish.

"Eternally."

"Oh." Her eyes rounded.

In the distance, a motor started up. The rumble carried faintly across the tableland. Not a truck-size motor. Probably an ATV.

Cam grimaced. "I think our sniper had enough of people shooting back."

Bree's full lips compressed into a thin line. She took a step out of the crevice, posture alert and rifle at the ready. Her exposure brought no response.

"I think you're right." She nodded at him as Cam stood from his crouch.

He walked toward the still, crumpled figure on the ground near the ravine wall, then knelt and placed two fingers against the man's neck. Cam looked up at the ranger and shook his head.

"He's gone, Ranger Maguire."

"Call me Bree. You've more than earned that right." Her stiff posture sagged. "I would have liked to bring him in still breathing, so he could answer publicly for his crimes."

"What did the guy do?" Cam rose and faced her.

"He is—*was* the leader of a particularly vicious gang of cattle rustlers. For the past ten months, his crew has been swooping into remote pastures, scooping up whole herds of cattle with semitrucks and leaving no witnesses behind. Lots of murdered ranch hands and hundreds of thousands of dollars of property stolen. People don't realize rustling is alive and well in the West or how lucrative slick operations can be. And then the night before last—"

She clamped her lips shut, and her face washed pale, revealing a scattering of light freckles across her nose and upper cheeks that her tan had concealed. Whatever she had been going to say choked her up considerably.

Cam stopped himself from pressing the issue. He was out of touch with the media reports more often than not, but no doubt, the next time he went to the coffee shop, someone there would let him know what had happened. Rural areas thrived on hearing and telling the latest news to keep life interesting. If he hadn't been camping out hunting strays for the past two days, he'd probably already know whatever had gone on.

He frowned at the rustler's body. "I've got a packhorse at the far end of this box canyon where I've been keeping the strays I've rounded up. We'll probably have to leave my kit behind and use old Myra to haul this guy out of here."

Bree didn't respond. She was staring at Waring's body also. At last, she stirred and looked up at him.

"I wonder who murdered this guy and took shots at us? Was someone trying to shut him up?" She pursed her lips and nodded her head. "Kind of confirms the notion we've been batting around at headquarters. Someone behind the scenes was coordinating the rustling activities—someone intimately familiar with where big ranchers pasture their stock."

"Someone Waring could expose." Cam completed the logical progression of thought.

Bree nodded. "I should go get the satellite phone in the pack on my horse. If you would wait here, I'll just be a minute, Mr. Wolfe."

"Call me Cam. You've more than earned the right."

He deliberately echoed Bree's words and added a grin to cover a sudden, surprising clench in his gut at using the name that went with his new identity. Usually, saying the name, which he actually liked better than his original, didn't bother him. It hadn't mattered the first time he'd identified himself to this woman before the shooting had started. Maybe the discomfort came from repeating the identity to an official of the law. Or maybe his unwelcome attraction to his neighbor added significance to the necessary deception. Except it wasn't really deception. Cameron Wolfe was now his legal name. He squelched the foolish introspection and maintained his grin.

"Cam, it is." She nodded with a smile and turned away. "We need to notify—"

Cam hissed in a sharp breath, cutting off her sentence. She whirled, gaze hunting for danger.

"*You* were the target." The words exploded from his mouth as his gut twisted. "The shooter was aiming to kill you first. If you hadn't moved to bend over Waring at the exact right second, you'd be dead now. The bullet took your ponytail clean off."

What was this woman not telling him about her situation? Could her predicament place him back in the crosshairs of ruthless criminals he'd turned his life upside-down to escape?

TWO

Bree's mouth dropped open as her hand darted up to grip the frizz that stuck out from the scrunchy at her nape. A shudder rippled through her and her heart hammered in her chest. She tore her hand away from the remnants of the thick mane of hair that had been her only vanity. The backs of her eyes stung and she blinked, swallowing against a sudden thickening in her throat. What was the matter with her? Why was she on the verge of tears over a physical attribute that would grow back over time? She should be grateful the bullet had not struck her in the spine.

Gritting her teeth and clamping fists that dug fingernails into her palms, Bree turned away from the concerned gaze of her too good-looking neighbor. Too good-looking? What was she thinking? It wasn't like her to moon over a guy she'd barely met any more than her pragmatic nature would normally mourn a hank of hair.

The tragic events of the past two days must be overwhelming her emotions.

Bree's boots crunched over the gravelly canyon floor as she rounded the corner away from the crime scene and marched toward her patient mount. Teton stood, steady and faithful despite the recent gunfire, gazing at her with dark eyes that seemed to hold the same concern as Cam Wolfe's. Was her uncharacteristic emotional state obvious even to an animal?

A pair of tears escaped the corners of Bree's eyes and tracked down her face. The salt stung the cut on her cheek with a welcome pain that brought her spiraling thoughts back in order. No, she wasn't weeping over hair, or an unwelcome attraction to a stranger, or even a close call with a bullet. Those things were distractions from the true grief of losing a dear friend. This type of normal reaction to the death of a colleague was exactly why she'd be required to see an assigned counselor before returning to duty. She had always considered the regulation a needless delay, but maybe there was a valid reason behind it.

"Good boy, Teton."

Bree patted her mount's silky neck then used the backs of her hands to swipe the moisture from her cheeks. After the gunfight the night before last, she'd been dry-eyed in a numb sort of way. Now, the dam was breaking, but she couldn't let loose yet. Law enforcement business needed to happen first. She pulled the satellite phone from her saddlebag and placed a call to headquarters. Shortly, her captain came on the line and she explained to him what had happened.

For long moments, deafening silence met Bree's terse recounting of events. Then Captain Gaines barked a wry laugh.

"Lieutenant Maguire, if I didn't know what a buttoned-down, by-the-book ranger you are, I'd suspect you went looking for trouble."

The semiamused tone tempered the tongue-in-cheek chiding of this sometimes maverick but highly effective ranger. Bree's spirits lightened.

"Just hunting for peace and quiet, sir. Trouble found *me*." She held back any reminder to her captain of her unheeded insistence to her colleagues that Waring would head for the Llano.

"Humph!" The wordless exclamation said her *told-you-so* had been read between the lines and noted. "And you say there's a civilian involved?"

"A rancher out hunting strays."

"Wrong place, wrong time for him."

"Or right place, right time for me. Cameron Wolfe saved my life, sir."

"Well and good. Well and good." Silence fell on the line again for several heartbeats. "Find a safe place nearby to hunker down and keep the rancher with you so we can get his statement. I'll have a chopper out there ASAP with a couple of crime scene techs and backup for you. Sounds like there are more bad guys on the loose than just the rustling crew we shut down the other night. Hopefully, they're satisfied now that Waring can't talk, but we still need to be cautious."

Bree bit her lip against voicing Cam's conviction that *she* had been the sniper's priority target. What reason could she give for the notion? She wasn't sure she believed it herself, despite the evidence of her missing ponytail.

A crunch of gravel beneath booted feet announced Cam's appearance around the bend of the wash. Bree nodded her acknowledgment of his presence and he sent her a questioning look with a tilt of his head.

"Ten-four, sir," she said into the phone. "We'll be here when the team arrives."

Cam made a wry face as Bree signed off on the call. "Let me guess. No moving the body, and we should make ourselves comfortable until the cavalry arrives."

She chuckled. "No cavalry in the rangers, and we're more likely to ride trucks and SUVs than horses these days, but yes, you have the gist of it. My captain is sending out a helicopter. I expect help to arrive within the hour."

Her neighbor scratched behind his ear and

huffed. "My cattle are thirsty and getting restless. You know what can happen if they take a notion to defy the cowboy and seek water. You'll have one trampled crime scene."

"Then we'd best go make sure the herd stays put." She motioned to Cam to head out.

Leading Teton, Bree followed him into the area where Waring's body lay. She didn't even have to tell him to skirt around the edge of the opposite canyon wall to preserve the crime scene. Bree kept her gaze on his moving figure and away from death. She'd had enough of that to last a lifetime. Many rangers went their whole careers without shooting someone or being shot. Bree was no longer among the number of those who hadn't shot someone, though, thankfully, the latter still applied.

Watching Cam stride along was no hardship. The guy moved like a seasoned hunter with the grace of a panther. Definitely an outdoorsman—another factor contributing to her unruly attraction toward him. Bree rolled her eyes at herself. Her psyche must be scrambling for something—anything—to keep her mind off the recent tragedy. Once she'd had a chance to process her grief, no doubt this fascination with her neighbor would fade. Besides, just because he wasn't wearing a wedding ring didn't mean he was unmarried or available.

They rounded another bend in the winding canyon and the lowing of restless cattle met her ears, along with the distinctive odor of a herd. Teton tossed his head and snorted with the cow horse's natural urge to dominate bovine waywardness.

"You'll get your chance, partner," Bree told her mount, who answered with a hot-breathed whiffle against her neck.

Another curve brought them within sight of the end of the dry wash canyon, a wide, rounded area ending in a sheer sandstone cliff striated with rosy Pleistocene-era rock deposits. Against the wall, about forty black Angus cattle mooed and milled, their hooves churning up a low-lying fog of the reddish Llano dust.

Near at hand, a rock-rimmed fire ring suggested Cam had camped there overnight, but the fire was well out. No smoke drifted from the ashes inside the ring. A pair of thick packs rested on their sides near the fire pit. Any tent or sleeping bag used by their owner was already stowed inside. Evidently, Cam had been preparing to move out when the confrontation with Waring occurred.

Beyond the ring stood a pair of horses, heads up and watching their approach. One was a short, stocky quarter horse mare, most likely the packhorse Cam had spoken about. The other was a magnificent chestnut bay stallion, also a quarter horse but long-limbed and sleek as a barrel racer.

Teton and the bay snorted at each other in unison. Bree held firmly to the reins on her mount. This was not a good time to start establishing a pecking order; a kerfuffle that could happen even between geldings and stallions. The mare gazed placidly at the newcomers, chomping a mouthful of dry grass. She plodded forward, coming between Teton and the stallion as if to say, "Not on my watch, silly boys."

Bree glanced at Cam, who stood, arms planted on hips, staring at the restless cow herd.

He turned his head and met her gaze. "I think we can hold them for a while if everything's calm. But if that law enforcement helicopter spooks them, we'd better get out of the way, and the crime scene will be toast."

Bree nodded. "I'll call Cap Gaines and have him notify the chopper not to overfly the area and to land at least a half mile away. The team will have to hike in from there. I know they'll be delighted."

Cam snickered, clearly appreciating her sarcasm.

Bree grinned at him and their gazes held. Heat, not related to the climate, crept up her neck onto her cheeks. Why couldn't she look away? Those gray depths held her and—

A nudge from Teton's nose broke the connection and Bree turned toward her saddlebags, the skin of her face boiling hot. *Get a grip, Lieutenant Maguire.*

Someone needed to tell her heart to stop fluttering in her chest. Hopefully, he had no clue the tough-as-nails ranger was crushing on him like high school was yesterday. The thought doused her in cold water.

Look what havoc had been wrought in her life because of a starry-eyed, youthful romance indulged and then gone sour too late to head off a marital train wreck. Another sort of burn began in her gut. A decade ago, her philandering ex-high-school-jock of a husband had abandoned his wife of fifteen years for another starry-eyed chicklet barely out of her teens. Apparently, Jared hadn't appreciated that Bree had stopped worshiping the ground he'd walked on, expected him to man up and do his share in the union, and was prospering in her career. She had matured and he hadn't. Simple as that.

Or not really.

The scars ran deep, and forty-three-year-old Brianna Maguire didn't do crushes. She barely did romance. Her last date lay far in the rearview and, until this moment, she hadn't minded that fact at all, despite her younger brother's un-subtle hints about getting back in the relation-ship saddle. Like the career bachelor should talk!

She pulled the sat phone from her bag and firmed her jaw. Gazing across her horse's rump, she noted that Cam had started saddling his bay. Good idea. They should be mounted while they attempt to keep the cattle calm.

As she began to key in the numbers on the phone, a bass *whump-whump* from the air above began to close in on their location. Sucking in a breath, Bree studied the cloudless sky, so blue it practically hurt the eyes. It was way too soon to expect the law enforcement helicopter. A private sightseeing chopper was possible, but to have one flying over this exact location was suspicious. Hopefully, the bird would soon change course.

Still gripping the satellite phone, Bree swung herself into the saddle to find Cam had done the same atop the bay. He headed his horse toward the small herd, crooning at them in a calming tone. The guy had a decent singing voice though Bree couldn't make out the words over the growing noise from the sky. She walked Teton closer to the cattle but refrained from breaking into song. She couldn't carry a tune in a bucket full of holes.

The helicopter noise continued to amplify and

the herd milled faster. Bree sent another look skyward. Nothing in sight yet, but the chopper was closing in on the canyon. Had the sniper sent reinforcements? Her heart began to pound in her chest, echoing the cattle's hooves.

Then the bird roared into sight, hovering directly above them. The cattle bawled and bucked as if coming out of their skins. With great bellows, they charged as a single living entity toward the exit from the box canyon. Bree couldn't have stopped them if she'd tried.

Bree gasped as the chopper's side door opened and a dark-clad figure pointed a rifle down at them. She whirled Teton and joined the fleeing melee. Coughing in the red dust cloud, amid the thunder of churning hooves and desperate huff of heaving bodies all around her, an instinctive prayer zipped through her mind, even though praying had ceased to be regular for her.

God, please don't let Teton lose his footing and fall.

The gunman was hardly the only threat. If her horse didn't stay upright with the herd, they'd wind up ground to paste between iron hooves and stony ground.

Swept up in the scrum of the charging herd, Cam leaned low over his horse's mane and pulled his neck bandana over his mouth and nose. His eyes watered and stung in the flying dust, but at least he could breathe without coughing. Next to him, a cow bellowed and went down, redness spurting from its back.

Cam's heart fisted. He hadn't been mistaken about spotting a shooter in the big bird's open door. They were being fired upon from above, and the herd provided no protection for him or for Bree. The helicopter could easily stay with the moving mass and pick them off until nothing remained standing.

Not today.

Saying a silent prayer that Bree was all right, Cam reined Rojo back. In its fear, the animal fought the bit, but Cam prevailed and the chestnut stallion slowed, allowing the herd to press ahead around them. As the last of the bellowing cattle darted past, Cam hauled his mount to a rearing halt and leaped from the saddle with his rifle gripped in his hand. The moment his boots hit the earth, he released the reins and the bay fled, neighing and bucking.

Don't blame you, pal. Flight was the animal's only recourse, but not Cam's. Not in this situation. A piece of him welcomed the fight. Craved it, since flight had been *his* only recourse not so long ago, and the position he'd been put in then had left residual anger he was still working to overcome.

Squinting into the sky against the dust swirling around him, Cam planted his feet and aimed the rifle skyward. As the reddish dust cloud began to settle, the hovering chopper took shape above. Cam pulled the trigger. The chopper moved at the last split second. Cam had missed the cockpit glass he'd been aiming for, but the bullet had struck sparks off the helicopter's undercarriage. The big bird jerked, not from the bullet, but no doubt from the pilot's reaction to the hit that would have reverberated through the cabin.

The shooter in the open doorway of the chopper swung into view. The guy's rifle stopped spitting bullets as he hung on for dear life against the sudden lurch of his aerial ride. Cam pulled the trigger again and embers arced from the bird's metal body near the open doorway. The shooter and his deadly gun disappeared back inside the chopper.

Cam was under no illusion the retreat would hold if the assault from below ceased. He pulled the trigger again and again, aiming for the cockpit glass to take out the pilot or for any part of the chopper that would disable it. The bird began to rise, attempting to get out of range.

Suddenly, a second rifle blasted from somewhere up the canyon, and the chopper's cockpit glass starred. Bree! And with an ace shot. Cam's heart leaped. She may or may not have hit the pilot, but if not, she'd certainly scared years off the person's life.

The chopper's whole body swung around, presenting its tail to him. The corners of Cam's mouth tilted upward in a grim smile as he took aim once more and pulled the trigger. Metal flew from the tail rotor assembly, and the bird stuttered in the sky. The back end fell, throwing the chopper into a spin. The pilot must still be able-bodied because the big bird sloppily righted itself and began to flee even as it lost altitude.

Moments later, the chopper slid out of sight, and then a loud *whump* carried across the plain. No flames or explosion followed the crash, but a helicopter blowing up on impact almost never actually happened. Cam wouldn't care to guess about the condition of the chopper's occupants, however.

He lowered his rifle and looked around. His camp had been utterly obliterated. The contents of his packs were strewn everywhere, most of the items ripped or flattened. The thunder of fleeing hooves had faded almost to nothing. His effort over the past week of rounding up strays was all wasted now, but at least he was still standing and unhurt. He couldn't say the same for the pair of inert cows lying nearby who had succumbed to rifle fire from above.

Heat flared within him and Cam gritted his teeth. Why were these yahoos trying to kill them, and who were they? He needed to find Bree and ask her some hard questions. Surely, she knew something.

He headed up the canyon, brittle scree crunching underfoot. This mess was the last thing a guy trying to keep his head down needed. Then a thought arrested him midstride. What if the attack had had to do with *him* and not her? If the cartel had located him, they'd have the resources to send in a chopper to take him out.

No. Cam shook his head and continued striding. The sniper who'd killed that Waring fellow surely had to be linked to the assault from the chopper, and he had shot at Bree first. *She* was the target, and Cam was incidental.

Probably.

What if the sniper was connected to Waring, but the helicopter attack was connected to *him*? A sour taste invaded Cam's mouth. He could hardly concoct a deadlier mess if two separate factions were vying to kill them. For now, he was going to go with the more probable deduction that all this led back to the ranger.

The likelihood that his identity had been exposed was slim to none. He'd covered his tracks via his own resources better than the Marshals Service had planned to do. *They* didn't even know where he was, and he wasn't about to inform the Texas Rangers.

"Cam"

Bree's shout jerked him from his dark introspection. Her trim figure rounded a bend in the canyon, and warm relief flooded Cam's system, flushing tension away. They were both caked in red dust and thoroughly disheveled, but alive and well.

Thank you, Jesus!

Cam hurried toward her. "You're a sight for sore eyes."

She swiped at her filthy face with the backs of her hands. "Literally sore. I could do with plunging my face into a rain-filled playa about now."

Cam snorted at the reference to a playa, a natural water catchment dug by the incessant wind on the plain and a unique feature of desert flatlands such as the Llano Estacado. "The cattle and our horses are no doubt headed for one right now—at least, once they calm down from their fright."

"We can look for them after the ranger helicopter arrives to give us a ride out of here."

"We?" Cam lifted his eyebrows.

"For sure. The least I can do is help you round up those strays again. Besides, I need to retrieve Teton. I'm sure my brother and some of the hands will join us, too."

"I won't turn down the help, but first we should go look to see if some survivor of that chopper crash isn't sneaking up on us to finish the job they started."

Her gaze lifted to scan the canyon rim. "Someone may be injured and need help."

"No doubt about that. As long as they quit using us for target practice, I'm game to try a little first aid. And a little interrogation, too." At her blossoming frown, Cam held up a hand, palm out. "Don't tell me to leave the questions to the professionals. I have a right to know what's going on."

"Fair enough." She jerked a nod, turned, and led the way toward the shallow end of the wash.

No more words were exchanged as they moved through the area where they'd confronted the rustler. Cam allowed himself only a sideways glance at the remains, and he appreciated Bree's wisdom in keeping her head averted also.

Within fifteen minutes, they had climbed out of the wash at its shallowest end and were standing on the level plain. The crumpled body of the attack chopper gleamed under the westering sun about a quarter mile distant. Belly on the ground, the big bird's landing struts had snapped off entirely. Another five minutes found him and Bree approaching the chopper on cautious feet, rifles at the ready.

Cam glanced toward Bree, already angling sideways, putting distance between him and herself so as not to provide targets close together. Good protocol. Also, the woman knew how to move noiselessly over the terrain. Not that they were exactly sneaking up on the location.

There was no cover on the grassy expanse around them. Not a rock. Not a tree. Much of the Llano was exactly like that—flat as the proverbial pancake, except for occasional stone upthrusts or the dry washes that often became dead-end canyons of the sort they'd been in. The rural prairie only naturally supported trees and vegetation other than grass and desert plants near the occasional springs or the seasonal playas that provided much-needed water for livestock, small game and pronghorn antelope.

Nothing moved around the crashed helicopter except for the lazy twirl of the rotors responding to the constant wind. Soon, they drew close enough for the ticking of the cooling engine to reach his ears. Then another sound intruded. Was that a groan?

Cam halted and darted a look at Bree. She returned the glance with a slight nod. He hadn't imagined the sound that could only come from a human throat. The opening of the chopper's side door gaped at them, dark as a cave mouth. The groan came again from the interior.

"Cover me," Cam told Bree as he edged closer.

"Nope," she said. "*You* cover *me*. This is my crime scene."

Cam gusted a sigh but bent his head in acknowledgment. She'd have to answer to higherups if she let a civilian usurp her duty as a ranger or get more involved than he needed to be. However, he could argue that he was thoroughly involved.

Dutifully, Cam held his rifle trained at the opening as Bree approached the door obliquely and peered inside. She bent down suddenly, yanked an object out of the chopper, and flung it behind her. A rifle.

"The shooter's alive in here," she said, "but unconscious. I don't know if the pilot made it. From the petite figure and dainty hand limp on the cyclic stick, the pilot appears to be a woman. She's slumped over, not moving."

Cam's legs swished through the yellowed calfhigh grass as he approached the downed helicopter. Bree shot him a scowl but didn't order him back. He needed to get a look at the shooter's face. There was a tiny chance he might recognize the guy, and if he could confirm it, he'd know he'd been found and would need to disappear again. If he didn't recognize the guy, he'd stay in limbo on what to do.

Standing on the opposite side of the open

door from Bree, Cam peered into the dimness. Gradually, his eyes adjusted and the features of the shooter's pasty, sharp-featured face became clear. No one he recognized, and the ethnicity did not match what would be expected of a cartel *sicario*—one of the ruthless hitmen employed by Raul Ortega, the drug boss who wanted Cam dead at any cost. Of course, Ortega could have gone outside of his own organization to hire the hit to shift suspicion off himself in any investigation, but Cam counted the probability of that move as very low. Ortega was not a subtle guy—he liked to use a hammer for every job—and he hated to outsource anything. Especially something of so personal a nature as his issue with the man Cam used to be.

If only Cam had no reason to know these details about such an evil man. But he couldn't change the past. He suppressed a shiver from a sudden chill originating deep inside his chest.

Another groan came from the injured shooter, who lay on his back, bleeding from someplace under his thick head of dark hair. Suddenly, the man's eyes popped open. He gazed around wildly then his stare fixed on Bree.

Shakily, he lifted a hand and pointed at her. "You!"

Cam's heart leaped. Was it wrong of him to feel relieved that the bad guy's recognition fell on Bree? At least now that he knew *he* wasn't the target, he could afford to stick around.

It probably wasn't his place, but he needed to help figure out why someone with serious resources like a helicopter wanted Bree dead and help do anything possible to put a stop to the danger. Of course, his unwelcome attraction to the lovely, courageous ranger played no part in his desire to protect. He would keep telling himself that until he believed it. No, he would attribute this compulsion to releasing pent-up frustration over the injustice of his own situation and his determination not to allow darkness to triumph once again.

The shooter's hand had fallen again to his side, and he had seemed to relapse into unconsciousness as his eyes fluttered closed. But then his hand moved subtly, not like an aimless twitch but in a specific direction. Cam scanned the man's form, straining to make out details in the dimness of the chopper's passenger compartment.

There!

The shooter was going for a knife scabbard at his belt. He planned to try to stab the woman leaning over him.

Pulse-rate suddenly in overdrive, Cam shouted a warning to Bree.

THREE

Cam's outcry reached Bree's ears even as she lunged into the chopper's belly and snatched the tactical knife away from the fumbling sniper. Venom blazed from the man's eyes and then they rolled back in his head as his body went limp. Unconscious for real this time.

Bree's jaw dropped at the frustrated rage that had radiated from the wounded shooter. She didn't recognize him. What had she done to inspire that kind of fury like she'd cheated him of a coveted prize?

Her mind sifted through the myriad arrests she'd made. Sure, any one of those people or their significant others might want revenge, but the timing of the attacks seemed so random if someone from her past was reaching out to hurt her now. It made more sense to connect this animosity to the recent shoot-out with the rustlers. Was there something she didn't know about the incident?

"I'll secure this guy and see what first aid I

can administer." Cam motioned toward the unconscious man. "Why don't you go around the
outside to the cockpit and check the condition
of the pilot."

Scowling, Bree jerked a nod and stomped
away. She wasn't angry with the new neighbor
who had been such a help, but she was furious with the situation. People were trying to kill
her. She needed an explanation for this vendetta
pronto.

The faint odor of spilled aviation fuel followed
Bree as she marched around the helicopter. At
the pilot's door, she peered through an opening left by shattered window glass. The woman
wasn't moving. Bree reached through the opening and put two fingers on the artery behind the
chinstrap of the pilot's helmet. A pulse throbbed
faintly beneath her fingertips. The pilot let out a
low moan. Alive. At least for now. A dent in the
woman's helmet hinted at possible head trauma,
though she'd likely be dead without the helmet's
cushion. There was no external hemorrhaging,
so Bree was hesitant to move her in case of spi-
nal injury.

Where was the ranger helicopter? Bree lifted
her head and searched the sky. A clean blue slate.
Not even a cloud in sight. She dropped her gaze
to the cockpit, scanning for weapons in case the
pilot revived and became hostile like the now-

unconscious sniper, but she spotted no guns or anything else that could be used to injure another.

Holding her rifle in the crook of one arm, she rejoined Cam, who was putting pressure on a wound at the side of the shooter's head. The man's feet were bound together by the shoelaces of his army-style boots and his wrists were fastened to each other by what looked like a dirty bandana. Bree huffed in appreciation of the ingenuity and wisdom in securing the suspect. Just because the guy was out of it didn't mean he would stay that way.

Cam lifted his head and nodded toward her. "The guy had a small handgun in his boot. I've relieved him of it, but I didn't find any other weapons. I don't think he has broken bones, but I have no way to tell if there's been any internal injury."

"The pilot's out, too. Possible head trauma and who knows what else. I don't want to move her. There's no cell service here, but if I had access to my sat phone, I could notify headquarters to send medical help. The unit is in my saddlebag, though, and Teton tore off with the herd as soon as I dismounted to shoot at the chopper."

"Rojo beat feet—er, hooves out of there, too."

"Smart horses. Rojo is a good name for a red stallion."

Cam flickered a smile in her direction. "He's got excellent bloodlines. I wouldn't have used him on hunting strays, but my mare is recovering from a slight hock injury, and the lone ranch hand I've hired so far took the gelding out to ride the fence. My herds—equine and bovine—are sparse until I can get to a stock sale and make some purchases."

Bree lifted an eyebrow. "You're going to raise horses, as well as cattle?"

"That's the plan."

"Then we'd better get after the missing animals as soon as we're done here. No worries about mounts for us. We've got plenty to spare at the Double-Bar-M."

"Thanks." Cam nodded. "I'll take you up on that offer. Now, what's the backstory with our deceased fugitive in the canyon and these two desperadoes here?"

Bree huffed through her nose. This man probably had a right to know about the law enforcement/rustler shootout that occurred the night before last. She gave him an abbreviated version. He listened with sober attention and only a frown and a nod at the part about losing her partner in the fray.

His demeanor signaled a savvy, steady temperament he'd already displayed in the tense situations they'd experienced. The only part of his response to her story that seemed a bit off was his apparent surprise and an odd hint of relief when she shared that the Espinoza cartel was behind the rustling ring. The impression of his reaction was too nebulous, however, to afford an opportunity for a question, so she pretended not to notice and continued her tale.

"And that's why I was out looking for Waring's trail." She finished with an exaggerated shrug as if she could unload her grief with that simple gesture. "Now, with this mess of the stampede and losing our mounts, the job is not done. If backup would only arrive, we could get on with—"

A faint but steady *whump-whump-whump* began to beat the air. Bree turned her face upward. There! A speck the size of a gnat in the distance.

"And here they come," she said. This desolate stretch of the prairie was about to turn lively.

A touch on her arm drew Bree's attention to Cam, who stood in the shadowed doorway of the downed chopper.

He motioned her to step through the door with him. "Let's be sure it's the good guys before we show ourselves."

Bree snorted. "You think the yahoos attacking us would be sending out a *second* helicopter?"

Cam's shoulder rippled in a shrug. "If they had one, they could have another."

"Point taken." She readied her rifle, stepped into the shadows beside her neighbor, and fixed her gaze on the approaching bird. Less than a minute later, the ranger star on the helicopter became apparent, and Bree let out a breath she hadn't realized she was holding. "It's them." She stepped out of cover and waved an arm at the law enforcement chopper.

Soon the bird lowered itself gracefully to the earth about twenty yards distant, sending rotor wash in their direction. Bree squinted against the grit and headed for the chopper. The side door opened, and a pair of her colleagues hopped out. Horn and Halliday, as mismatched a set of work partners as Bree's office afforded, met her halfway between the two helicopters.

Mitch Horn, a squat fireplug of a fortysomething man, waved toward the wreckage. "HQ didn't say anything about a downed chopper."

"What gives, Maguire?" Tall, lanky Dan Halliday's long greyhound face pulled tight in a scowl. "You okay?"

"I'm fine." She waved a hand in dismissal. "But we have injured aboard the downed chopper. Would one of you radio in for an air ambulance?"

Horn whirled on his heel and trotted back to the ranger bird. But his partner's body stilled as his cop gaze fixed on something beyond Bree's shoulder. She turned to find Cam approaching them with his smooth, big-cat stride.

"Chill, Halliday," she said. "This guy has saved my life at least twice today. He's a local rancher who went out after strays and wound up getting shoved into the deep end of fugitive apprehension and sniper fire."

The other ranger nodded. "Sounds like quite a story to tell."

Behind Halliday, a pair of jump-suited crime scene techs hopped out of the helicopter, bearing their kits in their hands. One of them waved at Bree. She waved back and then returned her attention to her colleague.

"Go ahead and get out your recorder," she told him. "You can take our statements while we wait for the medivac. Cam and I have strays to round up. I'm technically on leave, you know."

Halliday cracked a smile. "When has that ever stopped you from taking care of business? We were told you took Waring into custody out here. Where is he?"

Bree winced.

Cam came to a halt beside her. "Let's just say there's no need to get him to a hospital."

The other ranger frowned and pulled out his cell phone. In the field, witness and suspect statements were commonly taken through an encrypted app on State-of-Texas-issued phones.

"Let's hear it then," Halliday said.

The next couple of hours passed rapidly. The medivac came and went without interrupting the debriefing. Some conversations took place comfortably sitting in the shade of the ranger chopper with bottled water in hand, and some happened while traipsing around the area, including the dry wash canyon, touring ranger staff and CSIs through the various crime scenes. When they came to the spot on the canyon's rim where the first sniper had tried to kill Bree and had managed to eliminate Waring, the CSIs had a field day collecting bootprints and rifle cartridges.

"Amateur." Cam sniffed.

Bree eyed him sharply. "Why do you say that?"

"He didn't police his brass, and he ran away at the first sign of trouble coming back at him."

"I understand your deduction about the latter, but how would you know the significance of the former?"

Her neighbor shifted his stance from one foot to another and looked away quickly. "Guess it must be because I've read a few true crime books."

Cam's answer came a beat too late to ring genuine. Bree turned away with a soft frown. Her cop senses tingled. Though her new ranching neighbor had made himself a brave and faithful partner under fire, he was now hiding something. His behavior thus far had reflected good character, but the best of folks still had secrets. She'd let the matter slide for now, but whatever he concealed, Bree meant to find out—especially if it had anything to do with the rash of violence going on.

Cam brushed aside the pinch of discomfort at Bree's astute question about his knowledge of violent crime scenes. He'd slipped up in making his observation aloud. Maybe it wasn't a good idea for him to spend more time with her, even though he badly wanted to get to know her better. He hadn't felt interested in a woman since... He stopped the thought in its tracks. Best not to go there lest the pain overwhelm him. Bree would read the emotional upheaval in him, and then she'd have more questions he didn't want to answer—couldn't answer if he wanted to keep himself and others safe.

He turned to the stocky Ranger Horn. "Are you finished with Ranger Maguire and me here at the scene?"

Horn looked at Bree, who was studying footprints in the dust.

She rose and nodded toward her colleague. "What are the chances that we could hitch a ride to my ranch? It's a little off your direct route back to headquarters, but it would save us from having to contact my brother and get him to bring more horses. Cam and I would be twiddling our thumbs out here for hours."

"I think we can accommodate." Horn's gaze lit, and he smiled in a way that hinted at an interest in Bree beyond their working relationship.

Cam swallowed an inappropriate growl as they began moving as a trio for the helicopter. What was the matter with him? Why should he be bothered that someone else found Bree attractive?

The other guy was only a few inches taller than Bree's approximate five-foot-six, but twice as broad. Their ages were similar, and neither wore a wedding band, so the only obstacle to a romance might be any restrictions on dating between coworkers. Cam had no idea what the policy was in the rangers. For all he knew, Horn and Maguire were already an item. The cool dispassion in her gaze toward the other ranger seemed to negate that idea, and Cam's heart lightened. Perhaps Bree wasn't partial to the rough-hewn burly type and might consider a taller, slightly banged-up rancher type.

Then his spirits sank again. Why would she be any more partial to a scarred face with an even more deeply scarred heart? He'd be wise to let any attraction he felt for Bree Maguire die an unsung death—for both their sakes.

Soon the whole crew was strapped into seats in the ranger helicopter. Cam had a window seat with Bree settled in beside him. The thunder of the spooling-up rotors forestalled any conversation. Fitting a headset over her ears, Bree motioned at another headset tucked into a pouch on the back of the seat in front of Cam. He grabbed the headset and settled it over his ears. Not only did the padded earpieces greatly diminish the chopper's roar, but he now could listen in on conversations between the occupants.

When he tuned in, Bree was supplying the pilot with coordinates for her ranch. The big bird lunged into the air and headed in a direction south and east of their location.

Cam gazed down at the receding earth. His gaze stretched far and wide with only the occasional rock escarpment rearing from the flatness or shadowed canyons gouging into the land. It would be helpful if he could spot some trace of his herd and their horses, but nothing jumped out at him. They must be headed in the wrong direction. At least, that deduction would give him a clue about where to look.

In the far distance, cloud-ringed peaks of the Rocky Mountains punctuated the horizon. The Llano Estacado, sometimes translated as the Staked Plains, was one of the largest mesas on the North American continent, covering around 30,000 square miles with an elevation of flat prairie up to 5,000 feet above sea level right here in the northwest panhandle of Texas. The largest cities were Lubbock and Amarillo, thriving on the petroleum and natural gas industries. But most of the prairie supported dryland farmers and ranchers eking out a living in the arid environment through hard work and stubborn grit. The wide-open spaces and the ability to live quietly and mostly unnoticed among a sparse population were factors that had drawn Cam to choose this spot to hunker down and enjoy his privacy and relative safety. Today's events may have blown that aspiration sky-high.

"There!" Cam's heart leaped as he jabbed a finger in the direction of the ground below.

"What is it?" Bree leaned toward him, craning her neck to see out the window glass.

"An abandoned ATV."

Bree instructed the pilot to turn around and lose altitude to hover over the object.

Cam glanced at her taut face. "I'm pretty sure the sniper took off on an ATV. Could he have run out of gas or had a breakdown? If so, he's on foot, and we might spot him."

The ranger shook her head. "I'm inclined to think this is the fugitive Waring's escape vehicle. Running out of gas after fleeing the shootout was a distinct possibility for him. Probably why he was on foot when you encountered him.

I was following a blood trail he left when I came upon the face-off between the two of you."

Cam nodded. "Makes sense."

Bree straightened in her seat and asked the pilot to drop a GPS pin on the location to be investigated later.

Then she offered Cam a smile. "Good eye. I had wondered where his ATV had gone. Now we can wrap up his portion of this saga with a bow."

Cam stifled a snort. Too bad they still didn't have any idea why someone would be so desperate to take Bree out that they'd send not only a sniper but a helicopter to accomplish the goal. By the slight wrinkle in the ranger's brow, she was probably pondering the same issue.

The chopper flew onward and, not long later, descended toward a flat stretch of ground near a sprawling ranch site familiar to Cam from his meet 'n' greet visit with Bree's brother, Dillon, shortly after he'd moved to the area. Cam had deliberately set out to introduce himself to his immediate neighbors to establish normalcy that reduced speculation over the advent of a stranger into the rural area. As far as he could tell, the Double-Bar-M was a crack outfit with a neatly kept ranch house, bunkhouse, and barn, along with a modern machine shed and up-to-date ranch implements. Well-maintained fencing bounded pasturelands populated with horses and cattle. A ranch hand worked a horse in the corral by the barn, but no other human figure appeared to be in sight.

The bird touched down lightly, and Cam and Bree hopped out, crouching low as they scuttled beyond the whirling blades. Cam looked back to see Horn waving through a window at Bree. She jerked a nod at her colleague as the chopper rose. Cam might as well not exist as far as attention paid to him by the man. Yep, the guy had it bad, and Cam determined not to care as he followed Bree's brisk stride in the direction of the low-slung ranch house with its four dormers and front-facing porch. A tall man had emerged from the barn at the commotion of their landing and now ambled toward the house on a trajectory to meet them at the front door.

"Bree, what's going on?" the man Cam recognized as Dillon called as they neared each other.

Bree halted, and Cam with her, at the base of the two steps leading up to the wooden porch. The man who joined them nearly matched Cam in height but with a lankier build. His features resembled his sister's, but his hair was mahogany rather than auburn, and his eyes were blue.

"Wolfe." Dillon offered him an outstretched hand.

"Maguire." Cam accepted the handshake, their rough-hewn paws clasping firmly.

Then his upper-thirtysomething neighbor

turned to Bree, his initial question still hanging in the air.

Bree shrugged her shoulders and shook her head. "A mess, that's what. We tracked down Waring, and he's no longer an issue, but we ended up dodging bullets and shooting down a hostile helicopter."

Dillon's jaw dropped and his gaze darted from her to Cam and back again. "The two of you got involved in a gunfight and fought off an aerial attack? Whoa! That's wild even for you, sis. How did our new neighbor get caught up in this mess?"

Bree's teeth grinned white from a dusty face. "Let us clean up, and feed us, and we'll tell you. But then we need to head out to round up his cattle herd and our horses that got lost in a stampede."

Dillon flung up his hands. "Now you add a stampede to the excitement?"

"Long story." Cam chuckled despite the seriousness of the situation.

"I can't wait to hear." Dillon waved them to the door. "Get on inside. You two look like you've been wallowing in a dry playa."

Half an hour later, Cam joined Dillon and his sister in the spacious kitchen after enjoying a quick shower in the guest bathroom. Dillon had scrounged up a fresh pair of jeans and a shirt that didn't fit too badly. Sunlight streamed in through a wide window, illuminating a sturdy trestle table laden with a platter of thick roast beef sandwiches, a large bowl of potato salad, a plate of freshly sliced tomatoes, and an apple pie.

Cam's mouth watered. He didn't have to be invited twice to sit down and dig in. He ate ravenously as Bree began to fill her brother in about her day on the open range. Cam offered a remark here and there, but she did a clear, concise job with the story, reflecting a long history of writing after-action reports. To give him credit, Dillon seldom interrupted and then only with astute questions. The longer the account continued, however, the more furrowed the man's brow became.

"Someone is out to get you, sis," he declared at the end. "We have to find out who and put a stop to it pronto."

"I couldn't agree more," Cam said. He chewed and swallowed his last bite of a sandwich, wiped his mouth on a napkin, and then set the crumpled paper beside his plate as a tense silence fell on the group. The sudden burr of a ringtone sent a shiver through Cam, and he was pretty sure both Dillon and Bree jumped the slightest bit.

Bree cleared her throat as she swiped her phone from its holder at her waist and looked at the screen. "It's my captain."

She stepped out of the room and began a low-voiced conversation while Cam went to work on a healthy slice of pie. Though he strained his ears, he could make out no words, except Bree's tone grew slightly shrill at one point. As Cam was washing down the last bite of pie with a swig of iced tea, she returned to the kitchen, her freckles standing out on a face washed pale.

"What did you find out?" Dillon beat Cam to the question.

Bree cleared her throat. "The rustler I shot a day and a half ago has regained consciousness, though it's been confirmed that he may never regain the use of his legs."

Dillon grunted, wordlessly expressing how much he cared about the fate of a thief who stole the livelihood from decent, hardworking people and left the dead bodies of innocent ranch hands in their wake.

Cam couldn't say he disagreed.

"But that's not all." Bree's words began to come swiftly and forcefully. "The suspect has been identified as Emilio Espinoza."

A chill gripped Cam's gut. "Related to Alonzo Espinoza?"

Her gaze held steady on his. "Yes, he's the man's nephew."

Dillon planted his hands on the table, palms

down, and stood up. "Does this relationship tie in to why someone wants you dead, sis?"

Her gaze shifted toward her brother. "Apparently, a confidential informant told someone in division headquarters that Alonzo has put a bounty on my head."

The lingering savor of cinnamon and apple soured on Cam's tongue. Raul Ortega, the vicious head of the largest and most ruthless gang of drug and people smugglers on the American continent, sought Cam with lethal intent. Now, Bree was wanted by the head of the second-largest criminal organization. The same guy who was also a deadly rival to the Ortega cartel. The Ortega/Espinoza conflict had already racked up a sizeable body count on both sides of the border, as Cam knew tragically well. Each of these desperadoes was hunting a specific gringo to exact revenge, and the wanted pair—Bree and him—were now together in the same place.

In his wildest imagination, Cam couldn't have devised a more perfect storm. How could they hope to survive?

FOUR

Bree locked gazes with Cam. If the guy's skin wasn't so tanned, he'd probably look white as a Texas cloud. Even his lips had paled. Of course, she was shaken, too, but his reaction seemed out of proportion when they were barely acquaintances, and the threat wasn't against him.

What was going on with Mr. Cameron Wolfe? Secrets were in play, and she needed to find out what they were. But not here. Not now. She had enough experience interviewing people to intuit she'd get no plain answers from him. Besides, she'd be fishing in the dark. A little research into his background was in order before she started firing questions. That wasn't snooping; that was the due diligence of a law enforcement official.

Who was she fooling? She was distracting herself from her own situation by speculating about her neighbor. In law enforcement, personnel got used to being the focus of criminals' ire, but a bounty on her head? That was unusual.

Then again, cartel leaders possessed resources more significant than most bad actors.

"Sis!"

Her brother's outcry drew her attention to him. Dillon's fingers had formed white-knuckled fists. He'd gone fully as pale as their guest, but with reason. His sister's life was on the line.

"What did your boss suggest?" His voice rasped as if his throat had gone tight. "How are they going to protect you?"

Bree frowned. "They're not."

"I don't believe it." Dillon flung up his hands and then buried his fingers in his thick hair, kneading his temples. "You've been in law enforcement for twenty-five years and a ranger for what now—nearly two decades?"

"Nineteen years." A sense of unreality swept over Bree.

How had the time flown by so fast? She'd been in law enforcement for more than half her life, first in the state highway patrol right out of high school—the very year she'd married her ex—and then in the rangers.

"And they're not going to look after their own?" Dillon punctuated his question with the side of his fist hammering the counter.

"I didn't say that." Frowning, Bree dropped her gaze. "I can't do what they want me to do."

Cam rose beside her, eyeing her with a thin-lipped stare. "Let me guess. They want you to go into some version of Marshals Service protective custody, and you're not prepared to hide."

Pent-up air gushed from Bree's lungs. This guy got it. "Exactly." She trained a glare on her brother. "If I let some criminal force me out of my life, what message does that send to crooks everywhere and to my ranger colleagues? That a vendetta spooks the law?"

Dillon folded his arms across his chest and returned her glare. "How about that you'd like to go on living while said colleagues figure out how to end the threat? I can't lose you, too."

"I hear you, brother." Her insides warmed.

How blessed she was to have family who cared about her. Many people didn't have that precious gift. The sudden loss of their parents a few years back in the crash of their family's small airplane had made the two of them all each other had for immediate family.

"We're going to get through this," she said, "but you know I'd lose my mind stuck in some bolt-hole while others are out there taking care of business."

Dillon's whole body slumped. "Yeah, I get it, but that doesn't mean I have to like it."

"I should go." Cam retrieved his Stetson from where he'd placed it on a vacant chair and plopped it on his head. "You two have more serious things to figure out than rounding up a few stray cattle and quarter horses."

Bree swiveled toward him and planted her hands on her hips. "How were you planning to depart? It's quite a hike between here and your place."

Cam shrugged with a crooked smile that spurred an annoying *ka-bump* in Bree's heart. "Can you spare a cowhand to run me home?"

"And then what? Go after your cattle on foot? Didn't you say that your riding stock was depleted at the moment?"

"My mare should be healed enough to ride tomorrow."

Bree shook her head emphatically, swishing what was left of her hair. "I promised to help round up your animals, and I'd like to get Teton back ASAP. We stick with the plan to go after our livestock. We'll be out on the open range, and the bad guys won't know where to find me."

Her neighbor's smoky eyes bore into her. "They found you pretty handily earlier today."

"Cam's got a point." Dillon's gaze invited concession.

Bree thrust out her jaw. "I believe they were after Waring, like I was. Locating me was a bonus, and then *ka-blooey!* no ponytail."

Her lips trembled as she fingered the frizzy ends of her hair lying against her neck. She needed a haircut to even out her new short do—a truly inconsequential thought compared to living under a death sentence issued by the cartel.

Her brother sighed. "I know the set of your face. There will be no diverting you from your course."

"Then we'd best get to it." Bree smacked her palms together. "We're burning daylight."

A quick study of a satellite map on Dillon's PC revealed the closest wet, nonalkaline playa from the dry wash ravine where the shoot-out had occurred. The herd was almost certainly to be found where hydration and the accompanying plant life for food was available. A rough dirt road led across the Llano to within several miles of the playa, so they could drive a significant portion of the route.

With the help of a ranch hand, they got to work loading three quarter horse mounts and a pack mule into a trailer hitched to a heavy-duty pickup. Then they collected food, water, tents and camping utensils in pannier packs to be carried by the mule. These were thrown into the truck bed. They were fully prepared to spend the night on the range if the herd was not where they anticipated it to be and they had to keep hunting. But if they found the herd quickly, they could all be home by dark to enjoy soft beds for the night.

Bree threw herself into the busywork to keep

her thoughts from scampering like a rat in a maze over the horrible development of the bounty on her head. Her life had been upended in an instant. Was she right in resisting the safe course of action? Then again, how long would hiding stave off the forces that sought her? She couldn't think of a more miserable stopgap. No, she had to maintain her freedom and independence until she could figure out a way to end the threat entirely.

But how? The occasional speculative looks her new neighbor sent her as they worked tempted her to ask him what was going on in his head. Maybe he had some ideas. But why should he? The mystery of Cameron Wolfe kept growing deeper.

At last, they piled into the crew-cab pickup. Dillon drove and Cam rode shotgun. He'd offered to take the back seat, but Bree had ended the debate by climbing in behind her brother. Her neighbor had accepted defeat with a chuckle.

"Mr. Wolfe, you seem to have unvoiced thoughts about my situation," Bree said as they passed beneath the wooden sign mounted on twin posts announcing the Double-Bar-M ranch site.

Cam stirred in his seat but did not turn to meet her gaze. "My opinion shouldn't matter."

"I'm not looking for an opinion. I'm looking for insights."

"Please, share." Dillon's glance at the passenger said that he, too, must have noticed their guest seemed to be holding back comments.

Cam huffed. "You're in a tough position, Bree. Going into hiding feels confining and smacks of cowardice to a law enforcement personality."

"How would you know about that?"

He lifted a hand. "I'm just extrapolating here."

Why did Bree feel like Cam was deflecting? How much should she and her brother trust this guy if he was going to be slippery with his language? A chill slithered through Bree's middle. If she hadn't caught Cam in an armed standoff with Leon Waring, she might suspect he was in cahoots with the crook. But the moments she'd witnessed of the confrontation had the flavor of lawman versus criminal. That event, plus a few telltale comments, including the most recent, suggested Cam might have a law enforcement background. If so, why was he reluctant to say so?

Cam's head swiveled toward her, his gaze somber and piercing. "But you do have to weigh in the factor that going on about your life could endanger your loved ones or your coworkers by proximity to you."

Bree hissed in a breath as the words suckerpunched her. "You speak from experience?"

She read the yes in his eyes, but not a word passed his lips. A tic in the muscles of his jaw betrayed a battle going on inside him. Who had he lost? Or had it been his own life endangered by a situation beyond his control?

"Stands to reason, sis." Dillon let out a snort, seemingly oblivious to the byplay between Bree and Cam. "But don't let that thought give you a moment's pause. If you're not going into protective custody with the Marshals Service, then you're stuck with me by your side. Anyone after you will have to go through me. In fact, the more I think about it, the Maguires sticking together is the way it should be."

"No!" The word exploded off Bree's tongue. "I can't risk your life over my own stubbornness."

Silence fell as Dillon guided the truck into a turn from the paved road onto a washboard gravel byway that passed into the deep shade between a pair of stone outcroppings several times as tall as the pickup. Hunching into her seat, Bree stared out the side window as the stone walls slid past. Her stomach roiled with more than the jouncing of the truck. Everything in her rebelled against tucking tail and slinking away, but—

"Look out!" Cam's bellow filled the cab.

Bree whipped her head toward him as a great crash sounded against the windshield. Glass shattered and flew, a few bits stinging her cheek. A larger metallic object whizzed past her face but struck the rear window then fell away somewhere inside the cab. Even as objects zipped around the truck's interior, the men shouted, and a scream tore from Bree's throat.

Dillon must have reflexively mashed his foot on the brake because the rig shuddered and slowed. Scrabbling hooves banged against the floor and sides of the trailer, accompanied by shrill whinnies from the jostled livestock as the tires skidded on the packed earth. Metal groaned in protest as the front left corner of the pickup rammed solid rock, thrusting them to a sudden and complete halt.

Bree's head jerked forward and then slammed back against the headrest. Her senses spun and she fought the blackness edging her sight. She made an uncoordinated grab for the gun holstered at her side. It was her fault that her brother and her newfound friend were in danger. How had she been found already? And would she be able to defend them against the next projectile zipping into the cab?

Cam shook his head against sparkly stars lighting his vision from the jarring halt. Through the shattered windshield, dry heat invaded the cab. Odors of kicked-up dust and crushed mesquite pummeled his senses.

"Get down! We're under fire!"

At Bree's shout, he turned toward the rear seat. The ranger had drawn her sidearm and was swiveling her head this way and that, seeking the threat, but with limited visibility from her position in the back seat.

"We aren't being shot at," Cam said. "A drone crashed into us."

"A drone?" Dillon's voice emerged slightly slurred as he rubbed the side of his head where it must have banged against the side window. "Is that what came at us?"

Bree snorted. "Are you saying someone drove an unmanned, radio-controlled aircraft into our vehicle?"

Cam nodded. "I saw it swoop around the corner of the rock just before it hit us like a kamikaze."

"That's—" Bree blinked at him, mouth agape, like she was at a loss for words. Then her jaw closed and she shook her head. "That's beyond strange. You used an appropriate word, though, Cam. Kamikaze drones are an actual thing. If it had been one, it would have exploded on impact instead of shattering our windshield and itself." She turned her attention to her brother. "Dillon, are you all right? You sound woozy."

"I'm okay, sis." The younger man spurted a chuckle. "Just had my bell rung a bit. My brain is booting up again. I'd go check on the livestock, but I'm not able to get out of the truck. My door is too close to the rock face."

The vehicle jostled as animals in the trailer shifted their weight. Distressed whickers carried into the cab.

"They're alive, anyway, but who knows in what shape." Cam's hand closed around the door latch. "I'll go have a look."

"Wait!" Bree's sharp tone froze Cam in place. "We don't know if someone is out there waiting to take a potshot as soon as we emerge."

"I'll be extra cautious." He nodded. "But we can't sit and wait to be attacked further." Urgency twisted his gut.

"Agreed. I'll cover you as you move." Matte-black pistol gripped in her fist, Bree scooted across her seat to the rear passenger's-side door, lowered the window and peered cautiously out.

"Hold it." Dillon lifted a hand. "Pass me my shotgun from the roof rack back there before any of you venture outside."

Cam mentally kicked himself for leaving his rifle in the truck bed, temporarily inaccessible. At least he had his sidearm, like Bree, but all three of the weapons near to hand in this cab were short-range. Not much good if a sniper lurked outside to back up the drone.

Bree unfastened the shotgun from its secure rack and handed it to her brother. Dillon efficiently checked his load and then nodded at his sister.

Cam studied the pair, and his lips formed a grim smile. These two fit the bill for the Old West expression of "good folks to ride the river with." In other words, solid and dependable in danger and tough times. For someone like himself on the run from trouble, he'd been blessed with excellent neighbors. He could have found peace here in their company if all had stayed normal. But now he was being called upon to fight a battle not his own alongside them—a battle so *like* his own that he couldn't possibly turn away despite the risk of exposing himself to his enemies.

"Ready?" Cam drew his sidearm in his left hand as his right hand tightened on the door release.

"Ready," a pair of determined voices chorused, and a set of green eyes and a set of blue eyes lasered in on him.

Cam shoved the door open and hopped out, his boots sending puffs of reddish dust into the air. Head on a swivel, he searched the surroundings, including the tops of the escarpments bracketing them, but spotted no evidence of hostile presence. Of course, not seeing the enemy didn't mean they weren't there with all sorts of lethal aids like spotting scopes and high-powered rifles. But standing here with the meager defense of the truck door between him and a possible enemy approach would accomplish nothing.

Hauling in a deep breath, Cam transferred his pistol to his right hand and moved toward the trailer. Behind him, the sound of another vehicle door opening told him Bree had emerged to watch his back. Whiffling and snuffling noises from the stock accompanied his cautious progress. With another glance around, Cam stepped to the trailer doors and swung them wide. Equine heads turned to him, and the mule flicked agitated ears back and forth.

"As far as I can tell, they look okay," Cam said, "but we'll have to get them out to be sure."

"I'll give you a hand." Bree appeared around the corner of the trailer.

"And I'll use the sat phone to call for help." Dillon's voice carried from the truck cab.

"Roger that," Bree responded.

Cam met her grim stare. Neither one of them was under any illusion that assistance would arrive quickly at this remote location. The closest aide would come from the Maguire building site, where a grizzled cowpoke with a permanent limp oversaw the care of the ranch headquarters. All the other Maguire hands were out on the range. Dillon had introduced the on-site guy as Angus—Gus for short—the first time

Cam had met his neighbor when he'd stopped by to introduce himself. Gus could drive out with the spare pickup and trailer, but how much use he'd be in a potential firefight was unknown. Anyone with legal authority and firearms was a good hour away from their location.

Nope. They were on their own if further attacks happened.

Bree gave him a nod and Cam responded in kind. Then he stepped into the trailer, speaking in soothing tones to the troubled animals. One by one, he led the livestock out and tethered each one to the outside of the trailer. Dillon exited the passenger side of the truck and joined them, toting his shotgun in the crook of his arm and gazing warily around. Cam retrieved his rifle from the truck bed, checked the load, and hovered nearby on alert while the siblings ran their hands over scuffed hides and tested vulnerable legs.

Soon, Dillon stepped back from the mounts, now standing placidly by the trailer, the fright well past. "The mare has a shallow cut on her forelock from a flying hoof, no doubt, but nothing serious, though she's unrideable until it heals. They all seem a little worse for wear."

"Good to hear." Cam continued to scan their surroundings for threat.

Bree stepped closer to Cam. "Then you and I can saddle up, load the mule, and head out. Dillon can wait with the wreck and the lame horse for Gus to arrive."

"Now, hold on, sis." Her brother planted his fists on his hips. "You can't mean to carry on with business as usual. Somebody is out here flying drones, and they clearly knew right where we were headed so they could intercept us. As much as you hate the idea, I think you need to go into hiding. Let the Marshals Service help."

Bree scowled. "I'm safest out on the plain where I can see a threat coming a mile away or hide in endless meandering canyons. If necessary, I can lose myself in the wilderness where it would take an expert tracker to find me."

Her brother's face reddened. "Stop being so blasted independent. Your enemies aren't limited to ground pursuit. And think about me wondering and worrying where you are and if you're all right. These people have resources. They could hunt you down and keep track of you with another drone until shooters arrive. They could—"

"Hold on a minute." Cam interrupted Dillon's strengthening tirade. "I've had a few minutes to evaluate, and I don't believe the drone collision was on purpose. Think about it. Why would the operator destroy the drone when the utility of equipment like that is surveillance, not attack? We don't even know if someone from the cartel operated the drone. Could be anyone out to enjoy a new toy."

Bree snorted. "You don't really believe the innocent drone-flyer idea, do you?"

Cam shook his head. "Not really, but without proof, it's an idea we have to entertain. The drone was extremely high-end, with heavy-duty construction that broke through the windshield, rather than shatter on impact. But I tend to think that the collision was an accident. The stone outcroppings on either side of the road end only a few yards from where we were hit. I saw the drone swoop around the corner of the right-hand rock barely a second before sturdy truck met fragile flying object. The operator couldn't have known we were there. And now, all he or she can gather from any video feed is that their machine hit a ranch pickup with a couple of guys in the front seat. I suspect Bree's presence was hidden behind you, Dillon."

A short laugh spurted from Bree. "And the operator is now stuck explaining to whoever gives the orders how they wrecked their eyes in the sky. I like it."

Dillon crossed his arms over his chest with a scowl. "You do know that's only a theory."

"It's a sound one. Dill, you'll have to stay here and wait for assistance with the mare and the vehicle. Cam and I need to vamoose before anyone sees which direction we're going." Bree's face glowed, a grin stretching her lips.

If he didn't know better, Cam would think she relished the danger. More likely, she was relieved to grab on to a valid reason to take off into the wild rather than surrender to confinement. In that regard, the two of them were simpatico. If only the ploy could guarantee their safety, but fleeing into the Llano was a temporary solution at best.

The day was long gone when Quanah Parker's wily band of Comanche led the US cavalry on a near-hopeless chase across the vast plain sliced by rugged arroyos and winding canyons like the Palo Duro, the second largest canyon in North America. Today, pursuit on horseback had given way to helicopters and drones that were not limited by the terrain or the enormity of the prairie. The deadly criminals *would* find them. Then what?

FIVE

Bree gnawed her lower lip as she rode beside Cam across the semiarid tableland. The pack mule ambled behind them. Cam held its lead rope in his sturdy hand, and his head swiveled, gaze constantly searching the terrain. She was doing the same. This trek across the grasslands would have been pleasant and peaceful if they weren't under constant threat.

Saddle leather creaked and the sun-browned native grasses rustled, waving at them as far as the eye could see. The terrain hid depressions—dry washes called arroyos—in folds of the earth, but these were only discerned when one rode up on them. Occasionally, their passage flushed prairie chickens from their hiding places, and the birds scurried away, not taking to the air but warbling in alarm as they disappeared into the tall vegetation. Clumps of cattle grazed here and there, all Double-Bar-M brand since they were still on Maguire property. On the horizon, miles away, lazily whirling blades of wind turbines signaled human encroachment on the vast plain.

"Do you think I'm being stubborn and foolish to refuse protective custody?" Bree practically held her breath, awaiting the answer. Why did she care so much what this man thought? She hardly knew him. Then again, they had already developed the unique bond that only facing down deadly danger together could forge.

Cam frowned beneath the shadow of his hat brim. "Stubborn, yes. Foolish?" His broad shoulders rippled in a shrug. "I can't say I blame you a bit for your choice. Hunkering down in a hidey-hole waiting for who knows what event to set you free from threat in the nebulous future doesn't sound like any way to live. If there was a plan in place to force Alonzo Espinoza to lift the bounty on your head, then I'd say for sure take the temporary arrangement."

"But there is no such plan." Bree scoffed. "How can law enforcement in the US force a cartel leader in Mexico to drop a vendetta?"

"That is a priceless question, and I have no answer. Yet."

"Are you expecting the solution to drop like rain out of the sky?"

Cam awarded her a sidelong look, his expression unreadable. "Let's just say I've submitted the question to the One who has all the answers. When He gets back to me, I'll let you know."

Scowling, Bree guided her horse around a prairie dog hole. The situation she was in seemed like a field pocked with hidden prairie dog holes. One misstep would bring disaster. Maybe she'd already made the biggest misstep of all in going her own way rather than entrusting herself to the legal system she served. If she was making an error, would God protect her from the consequences of a bad decision?

Yet, hiding away indefinitely felt like a worse decision. Like making herself a sitting duck if—no, *when* killers spurred by the bounty on her head located her. Then the guards on duty around her would be endangered, also, as the concerted weight of cartel heavies fell on them. Bree sucked in a deep breath of air laden with the piney-fresh scent of nearby juniper shrubs. No, she was making the right choice. For now.

"Here's the edge of Double-Bar-M land." Bree pointed to a barbed-wire fence line with a gate situated maybe half a football field distant from them.

Soon, they unlatched the gate and moved over onto Cam's Diamond-W property.

"My livestock and your horse should be a few miles west of here." Cam spared Bree a swift grin as they urged their mounts into a slow jog. "Let's go get them. We can drive the herd to the pasture closest to my place in time for supper. I've got spare bedrooms in the house. You can bunk there out of sight and away from home. By now, hostile surveillance might be set up around the Double-Bar-M ranch site, waiting for you to show your face."

"Do you think we got out of there before any of the bounty hunters had eyes on the place?"

"I do. Otherwise, a drone would not have been sent out looking for you. The enemy would have intercepted us in force on the road because they saw you leave the ranch with us."

"Fair deduction. I'm pleased to accept your hospitality. Let me call Dillon to let him know the plan and check how things are going with him."

Bree pulled the satellite phone from the saddlebag. The call went through, but the ringtone went on and on with no answer. Holding a tight rein on the worry that wanted to gallop away with her, she mashed the off button. Was everything okay with her brother?

"No answer?" Cam's gaze rested gently on her.

Bree's gut clenched.

Her neighbor offered her a half smile. "You do know he must have his hands full getting the equipment wrangled out of that narrow roadway. He might not be near his phone."

She let out a long breath. "I know you're right, but I'm tense as a bowstring."

"I don't blame you. Head back there if you want to. I can handle the stock."

Bree shook her head. "It's probably more dangerous for Dillon if I'm nearby."

"So, you're hanging around *me* instead?" Cam grinned. "After all, I'm just the expendable neighbor." The twinkle in this eye let her know he was teasing.

A reluctant laugh spurted between her lips. "You've got me there. Events have sort of gotten away from us, and we're scrambling from one thing to the next. Why are you helping me?" The question burst from Bree's lips. "I mean, you're risking yourself. Why?"

A cavernous silence answered her as his figure stiffened in the saddle. Finally, he angled a grim look in her direction.

"Isn't that what neighbors do? Help each other?"

"This sort of help goes beyond neighborly courtesy."

Cam's complexion darkened and his eyes narrowed. "Let's just say I don't let it stand when people take shots at me, whether I'm the main target or not." His voice had deepened to a low growl. "That experience makes me want to do anything I can to deny these crooks what they want."

Bree opened her mouth and then closed it again. He was right. He'd been in the crosshairs, too, more than once. Her proximity was toxic, but the threat seemed to make Cam dig his heels in deeper. Some folks were like that, but often, they were the sort of people who gravitated to careers like law enforcement or the military. Had Cameron Wolfe always been a rancher? She knew next to nothing about him, but that didn't mean she was comfortable endangering him, and certainly not risking her brother. Simply by being related to her, he could be targeted as a pawn of the cartel to get to her.

Bree's heart did a little jump in her chest. Maybe Dillon and she should go into protective custody together. She repressed a derisive laugh. Dill wouldn't allow himself to be yanked from his life and hidden away any more than she would. Next time he pressured her to accept the offer of protection, she'd point out that little fact to him.

But where did this thought process leave them? In limbo. A highly uncomfortable place to be stuck, that's for sure. For now, she'd have to follow Cam's advice of coping with this situation one step at a time.

The first step, round up those stray cattle and retrieve her horse.

And there they were, near a halo of lush, green growth surrounding a pale blue stretch of water that covered less than an acre of ground. Last week's unseasonal downpour would have filled the playa's shallow basin. But late summer's unrelenting heat nibbled swiftly away at the wetness, leaving cracked and baking mud around the edges as the water receded. Within a few more days, the wetness would be evaporated. The herds and wildlife would then be dependent for water on the few rivers that cut through the Llano or on occasional springs fed by the underlying Ogallala Aquifer. That's why ranchers and farmers had installed water tanks here and there across the plain.

As if in silent communication, Bree halted her gelding simultaneously with Cam.

The herd and handful of equines milled around the edge of the water, churning the mud. Why were the animals restless? They should be content with their environment. The slow, quiet approach of riders would not have stirred them up.

Bree rose in her stirrups and narrowed her eyes on a distant dust cloud roiling across the plain on a clear trajectory toward the herd. She went quiet and strained her senses to see or hear what approached. The rhythm of hoof beats lacking any engine growls suggested another herd racing for the water. Why were they coming on so fast, almost like the animals had been spooked or were being driven? Either possibility brought up another host of questions, like what had spooked them or who was driving them—unanswerable at this point.

Bree glanced over at Cam, and he met her gaze with raised eyebrows.

"We should intercept the coming herd and slow them down so the whole bunch doesn't stampede."

"We'll have to hustle to swing around to the far side of the playa before that second herd arrives."

Cam jerked a nod and released his hold on the pack mule's lead rope. "Let's get to it."

By the time she and Cam reached the far side of the playa, the incoming herd had grown much closer. The cloud of reddish dust still obscured most details, but the distinctive grunting of cattle on the move informed Bree's ears. A mass of dirty-brown bovine bodies undulated across the plain toward them. But a different silhouette of horses and riders trailed behind. At least three cowboys.

Cam let out a wordless growl. "Who in the world is driving cattle across my property?"

His shouted question reached Bree's ears above the rumble of the herd and echoed the question in her mind. She'd scarcely formulated the thought when a distinctive crack echoed across the plain, drawing surprised bellows from the herd in front of her and the one behind her.

A whip?

The sound came again, and something like a bee whine zipped past her ear.

Not a whip. A gunshot.

The approaching riders were firing at her and Cam—or maybe just her. Heat roiled through her veins. Being targeted was getting very old, very fast.

Pulse hammering in her throat, Bree leaned over the neck of her horse, reached for her saddle scabbard, and drew her rifle. As she brought the weapon to bear on their assailants, her mount stumbled beneath her, throwing her forward. Then the animal fell headlong. A shriek escaped Bree's throat as her feet left the stirrups and she went airborne.

Shouting Bree's name, Cam swerved his horse toward the fallen rider, who lay flat on her back and unmoving on the ground. His heart filled his throat. Pulling up beside her prone figure, he swung out of the saddle even before his mount came to a full stop.

Bree stirred, blinked, and sat up. A gush of pent-up oxygen left Cam's lungs. She was alive, at least. Assessing any injuries would need to wait. That other herd was bearing straight down on them, and they needed to get out of the way. Not to mention continuing to dodge bullets.

The question of who those other riders might be was settled when the trio opened fire on him and Bree. Nothing legitimate about them. They were rustlers. Or maybe bounty hunters, intent on collecting the price on Bree's head and using the small herd as cover for their approach.

As Cam bent toward Bree, she gripped his arm and struggled to her feet. Despite the jarring fall, she still clutched her rifle in her other hand. Cam steadied her with an arm around her shoulders.

"We've got to get out of here," she mouthed more than spoke aloud. No doubt she was still struggling to breathe after doing a cartwheel and slamming into the hard earth.

Cam darted a glance around. Bree's horse was hobbling away from them, clearly lame. The animal had probably stepped in a prairie dog hole. His jaw firmed. They'd have to ride double on his mount. Then, a whicker behind them drew his attention. Her gelding, Teton, approached, single rein dragging on the ground, the other snapped off short. No doubt stepped on by sharp hooves in this morning's stampede.

As one, Cam moved with Bree and got her on the palomino's back. He had small doubt the animal was sufficiently trained to respond to leg commands, even though Bree would have only one rein in her hand. Of necessity, Cam ignored her pained groans accompanying the effort, but his heart squeezed in on itself. Then he leaped aboard his own borrowed mount, and together they raced out of the oncoming herd's path. A pair of thunderclaps let them know those hostile riders were still shooting at them, but it was extremely difficult to hit a rider on a moving mount while astride racing mounts themselves.

Provoked beyond measure, he lifted his rifle and returned fire, not expecting to hit anyone but hopefully encouraging the attackers to back off. One of the enemy riders flung up his hands and toppled off his mount. Cam's jaw dropped even as Bree opened fire beside him. Neither of the remaining attackers fell, but they whirled their mounts and raced away across the plain.

Not a very gutsy response from ruthless cartel *sicarios*, but standard for crooked cowpokes out to make a fast buck from stolen livestock. It was possible the crooks had no idea Bree Maguire was one of their opponents. But perhaps that was just wishful thinking on his part…

Coughing against the settling red dust, Cam trotted his mount over to Bree, who had brought Teton to a halt. She sat slumped on his back, echoing Cam's coughs.

"Where are you hurt?" he asked.

Bree grimaced at him from a dusty face. Even

caked in dirt, this woman was appealing. Cam squelched the unwanted attraction. She wasn't likely to be regarding his grimy, scarred face with similar interest.

"Where *don't* I hurt would be an easier question to answer, but I'm pretty sure nothing is broken, and I'm not concussed. However, I'll probably be one big bruise in the morning. Let's go check on the fallen rider."

"My thought exactly."

They guided their mounts together at a fast walk toward where a riderless horse had stopped to graze and a human figure lay unmoving a few yards away. She kept her rifle at the ready, as did he.

"That was one tremendous shot."

Cam met Bree's sidelong glance. "A major fluke, you mean."

They stopped their mounts near the crumpled figure, who stirred and groaned but didn't open his eyes. Red blood pooled near the guy's shoulder and stained his plaid shirt in the same area, but nothing life-threatening. Something like a fist unfurled from around Cam's heart. He hadn't killed the guy, after all, which was one burden off his conscience. Plus, maybe they could get some information out of the rustler if he came around enough to talk.

"Keep him covered," he said to Bree as he

swung off his horse. "I'll get the first-aid kit and check him out."

"Gotcha." She kept her rifle trained on their wounded attacker.

Moving cautiously with one eye on their prisoner, Cam retrieved the medical kit from his saddlebag and then knelt beside the downed range rider. The man was paunchy and scruffy, not an impressive physical specimen. His grizzled hair betrayed upper middle age, past his prime, and his threadbare jeans spoke of a cowpoke in poor financial circumstances. Were money troubles the reason why he'd hooked up with a rustling outfit? Regardless, that was no excuse to be shooting at other people.

Compressing his lips, Cam got to work checking out the man's wound. Turned out to be a through-and-through just below the clavicle. No bloody froth lined the guy's lips, so likely the lung was not nicked. What kept the guy unconscious seemed to be the knock his head had taken against a rock when he'd landed on the ground. Strangely enough, the skin had barely broken, with minor bleeding, yet a growing knot suggested a probable concussion. There wasn't much Cam could do about the head injury, but he disinfected both sides of the shoulder wound and staunched the bleeding with compresses.

"This guy needs professional medical attention, but in my nonprofessional opinion, if his head injury isn't too severe, I think he will recover."

A heavy sigh answered him. "I can't believe I'm calling for helicopter emergency services twice in one day."

"I'm just thankful the callout isn't for either of us."

"I can get on board with that idea."

Cam checked the grizzled cowpoke for any additional weapons to the rifle the guy had been firing at them but found only a buck knife, which he took away and pocketed. Then he finished bandaging the man's wounds while Bree talked on the satellite phone. She called for aid and then reached out to her brother to get and give updates. This time, Dillon answered, which brought a smile to Bree's face.

From her end of that conversation, Cam inferred that salvaging the wreck of the truck and trailer had gone well. When she started telling him about their situation on the range, the tone of the conversation changed drastically. Her brother's fuming shouts reached Cam's ears, though he couldn't make out what was said. Not that he blamed the guy for getting agitated when his sister kept going from one dangerous situation to the next.

Bree brought the conversation to a firm conclusion, informing her sibling she planned to finish what she and Cam had come out there to do. The woman was the definition of stubborn. If the situation weren't so serious, he'd be tempted to grin in appreciation of a kindred spirit.

Creaking saddle leather let Cam know Bree was dismounting from Teton. He peered over his shoulder to find her approaching her lame mount, who stood nearby, head down. She reached for the horse's bridle, and Cam caught on that she would be switching the intact headgear onto Teton. Cam returned his attention to the downed rustler. A few minutes later, Bree appeared at Cam's side, leading Teton, just as he rose to stand over his patient. The man had begun to groan and flutter his eyelids.

Cam planted his hands on his hips and frowned down at the guy. "I should look through his saddlebags and see if he's carrying some kind of identification. When I looked him over, I didn't find a wallet."

"No need." Bree scowled. "I know this guy. Ben Trout. Born and raised on the Llano. He's bad news with a sad story. Started out young as a decent cowhand, but too much drink and foolish choices in the company he kept led him down a crooked path. Trout's one of the few rustlers that slipped the net during our tragic shootout the other night."

Cam snorted. "I'm surprised he hasn't found a deep hole to hide in, rather than prancing across the range stealing more cows. He must be desperate for money."

"Desperate, for sure. Despite the rustlers' recent losses—or perhaps because of them—the cartel may be holding them to a quota of stolen beef."

"That's cold." Cam snorted. "But typical."

Bree jammed her hands onto her hips, mimicking his posture. "I'm done letting your cryptic comments slide, Mr. Wolfe. If you want me to keep on trusting you, tell me how you seem to know so much about how criminal cartels behave. And don't put me off with any flippant remarks about watching crime documentaries on TV or the internet."

Cam's mouth went dry as he met her glare. What could he tell her? His glance flicked toward the groaning man on the ground. The rustler's eyes remained closed, but he might be hearing every word he and Bree spoke, and despite being headed for the hospital and then to jail, Trout could easily find the opportunity to share his information with someone. Possibly the wrong someone. At the same time, clearly, the tough ranger was through allowing him to skate along unquestioned about his background.

He couldn't mention being a former DEA

agent. If he made that claim, she'd check him out and discover no Cameron Wolfe ever on the DEA roster, which immediately would destroy all trust between him and Bree. Worse, alarm bells would sound throughout the law enforcement community. Official attention would come and expose his identity to the Ortega cartel. He'd have to disappear again. His stomach curdled at the thought.

It had ripped him apart to choose the flight route when fight was his natural instinct. But the overwhelming forces arrayed against him at the time, as well as the emotional pain of his losses, had forced him into what he'd regarded as an honorable retreat. He'd gone into hiding in plain sight and on his own terms. But now, even if he possessed the resources to turn himself into someone else again, he didn't think he could bring himself to do it. He'd done all the retreating he could stomach. Stubborn, yes, just like Bree.

He lost himself in her earnest green gaze, and his heart did a little jig. Despite any negative consequences to himself, for the first time in a long time, a part of him ached to share the whole story with someone. No, not just someone—this brave woman staring expectantly at him.

But if he said too much, he would not only risk himself but double the danger to her—and who knew how many innocents—when the Ortega enforcers showed up and inevitably clashed with the Espinoza *sicarios* in their hatred of each other and eagerness to take down their targets. How selfish, not to mention foolish and irresponsible, would such careless transparency be? But he *had* to tell her something, and it would need to be enough of the truth to satisfy her.

God, guard my mouth and give me wisdom.

SIX

Bree all but held her breath for Cam's response to her insistent question. Color ebbed from the man's cheeks, and his gaze tore away from hers as he appeared to study their surroundings. Then he glanced back at her, but the eye contact bounced off and fell to the injured man on the ground. Cam's lips thinned, and he jerked a nod toward no one as if coming to some sort of conclusion.

"I cooperated with law enforcement on a certain project that ended well for some, but not for me." He heaved a deep breath. "I was engaged, but…things happened that changed me. The cartel mess brought tragedy, and—well, the wedding never happened, so I moved away to start over."

The raw pain on Cam's face ripped at Bree's heart. She shouldn't have pried, and yet, for her own assurance, she'd had to understand what was going on with her neighbor. Still, he was telling her the bare bones of what must be a complex and difficult story.

"I'm sorry." Her words came out gently. "Was your fiancée killed?"

Cam grunted as if he'd been struck in the stomach. "No, she survived, but she was an emotional wreck. She fled with important unresolved questions between us. In some ways, that consequence has been more complicated to properly mourn." His mouth twisted in a grimace.

"Very well, Cam. I'll stop badgering you about your personal business. You understand that I need to know anything that impacts my current situation."

"I get it, and I appreciate your discretion."

If the guy looked any more relieved by her backing off, he'd flop onto the dirt like jelly. The reaction sparked her curiosity more than ever, but as she'd promised, she put the matter on a mental shelf. For now.

The cowboy on the ground moaned and started mumbling something. Bree squatted beside him and Trout's eye popped open. He fixed her with an inky stare that started out bleary and then snapped into narrow-eyed focus.

"You!"

"Yep, Texas Ranger Brianna Maguire. And you're under arrest, Ben Trout, for cattle rustling and attempted murder." She briskly informed him of his rights. "Do you understand what I've said to you?"

Trout snorted a phlegmy laugh that ended in a wince. "I got it, all right. But if I'd known it was you I was shootin' at, I'd have made sure to aim my rifle better, instead of just tryin' to scare you off as if you was a hired cowhand. You're worth a pile more money than them scraggly cows."

"I've heard." She infused her tone with enough flatness to hide the cold pang that shot through her at his words.

It was one thing to be told by her boss about the bounty on her head. Quite another to hear it spoken with venom from an enemy.

The rustler squirmed and tried to sit up, but Cam put a boot atop Trout's good shoulder. "Stay down unless you want to be cuffed."

Bree spread her hands. "Sorry, I don't have cuffs on me for this roundup, but I do have a few zip ties." She grinned down at the prisoner, who looked away with a scowl.

"I need a doctor." A whine replaced the harsh tone.

"Air ambulance is on the way," Bree told him. "In the meantime, you can tell me what you're doing trespassing on Diamond-W land, driving a herd of Cameron Wolfe's cattle, and shooting at random people you just basically admitted you had not identified."

The man sucked his lips between his teeth and then smirked. "I don't have to say nothing without a lawyer."

"That's right. You don't. But that doesn't mean your buddies we arrested a couple of nights ago aren't singing up a chorus with your name in the lyrics."

Since she was on leave, Bree was throwing out speculation on what the interviews were yielding with the captured rustlers. But Trout didn't need to know she was temporarily out of the loop.

"Since you've got this guy under watch," Cam said, "is it okay if I go over to the herd, secure Rojo, and check the condition of the cattle?"

Cam's question drew Bree out of her inner mulling, and she gazed up at him. He was frowning and scanning the horizon, clearly still uneasy about their situation. She didn't blame him. Her own senses remained on high alert.

"Absolutely." She offered him a nod. "This guy's just a distraction from what we came to do. As soon as he's out of here, I'm right with you."

Cam nodded soberly. "If you feel you need to head out on the helicopter with the prisoner, I totally understand."

She shook her head. "I'll zip-tie his wrists to the gurney and make sure someone from the rangers division at the other end to receive him, but I'm staying out here with you."

"And away from the clutches of anyone who might want to corral you into doing something you don't want to do, like going into protective custody." Cam grinned down at her.

Bree grinned back. This guy got her.

He tipped his hat and then climbed onto the mount that Dillon and she had lent him.

Bree returned her attention to the rustler, who appeared to have resigned himself to his enforced repose on the ground. Or maybe it simply hurt too much to move. She settled in, cross-legged, beside him, keeping her rifle in her grasp.

"So, tell me more about this bounty Alonzo Espinoza has allegedly placed on my head."

Trout pursed his lips as if considering the request. Probably figuring out what to say that wouldn't incriminate himself further.

"Don't know much. Just that the young fella you shot and crippled was Alonzo Espinoza's sister's son, and the big cheese's choice to lead the cartel after he retired."

Bree snorted. "I haven't heard of a cartel head yet who made it to retirement alive and unincarcerated. It's a high-risk occupation—as is being a rustler."

"Just sayin' what I heard. Got that? Hearsay only. Nothin' criminal."

"No, but you being aware of the details reflects the sort of people you hang out with."

"Are you judging my friends now?"

"I'll leave the *judging* to the actual judge on the bench. You'll be facing one soon enough."

An uneasy silence fell and a sullen look took up residence on the rustler's expression.

Cattle lowed softly and hoof thuds increased behind her near the playa. A baritone voice, singing a cowboy melody and carrying a tune quite well, met Bree's ears. The familiar odors of livestock and ancient, sunbaked Llano dust filled her nostrils.

Bree's gaze found Cam's tall figure, now mounted on Rojo and guiding the stallion, slow and easy, through the livestock. His head turned this way and that, inspecting the condition of the herd. After being shot at and stampeded, injuries needing treatment were likely and had to be identified and assessed.

Bree's brows drew together. Her new neighbor, encountered so dramatically this morning, exhibited all the earmarks of an experienced and caring rancher. Why did she continue to think his main occupation had been something else until recently? Maybe because of how cool he was under fire. But if it were so, why wouldn't he tell her?

Yet, more troubling to her personally, how come in so short a time, she felt like she'd known Cameron Wolfe forever and would like to go on knowing him for an eternity more? That kind of instant crush didn't happen to Bree Maguire. She knew better. At least, she had until her heart started trying to override her good sense. Bree shook her head as if warding off a pesky horsefly.

Cam must have felt her eyes on him because he turned his head in her direction. He lifted a hand in greeting and she responded the same.

Time passed as Bree kept an eye on the captured rustler and the surrounding terrain for any return of the crook's buddies, perhaps with reinforcements. The westering sun peeked beneath the wide brim of her cowboy hat, though a fresh breeze mitigated some of the heat. Cam continued to work with the cattle, occasionally resuming his crooning. Beneath all the sensory input, her nerves thrummed in anticipation of the sound of an approaching helicopter.

When it came, she physically jerked and rose to her feet, eyes piercing the horizon for a sight of the big bird. Her skin prickled like she was swathed in a blanket of tiny needles, and her grip tightened around her rifle. She whistled Teton over and mounted up.

If she and Cam had to run, they'd do better on horseback. The memory of this morning's chopper attack loomed all too fresh in her mind. The last time they'd expected the good guys to show up from the air, the bad guys had arrived instead, and she and Cam had barely survived.

Rotor rumble began to drown out the thud of milling hooves and lowing of livestock as Cam continued his inspection of the herd. So far, he'd discerned only minor wounds among the cattle that could be treated in the pasture. He might have the vet come out to look at his old pack mare, who sported an angry red bullet graze across her flank. She wouldn't be carrying a load for a while. Cam lifted his head skyward. The big bird made a speck in the deepening blue sky of impending dusk and the speck grew bigger by the second. The hairs at the base of his neck prickled. He wouldn't relax until he spotted the hospital logo on the chopper's side.

Still crooning to the herd so they would remain calm while the chopper landed, he gradually began urging his mount out of the press of animals and toward Bree, who had remounted Teton. Cam stopped his horse within speaking distance of Bree but far enough distant that the pair of them wouldn't make convenient bunched-up targets. Rojo pranced and snorted, muscles rippling beneath his sleek, red hide. If the need came to run, the stallion was eager to go.

Bree spared them a glance but mostly divided her attention between her prisoner and the sky.

The scraggly rustler moaned loudly as he hauled his body into a hunched sitting position. Bree's voice admonishing the man reached Cam's ears as an indistinct murmur—the specific words lost beneath the growing roar of the helicopter. Then Cam made out the markings on the side of the big flying machine and the fist around his heart unclenched.

"It's the emergency chopper."

His cry drew Bree's head toward him and she nodded, a smile breaking out over her face. The bird eased to a gentle landing far enough distant that the rotor wash dwindled to a mere breeze by the time it reached their location, and the herd would not be spooked. Almost immediately, a pair of uniformed emergency medical technicians hopped out, bearing a stretcher between them, one with a medical pack in her opposite hand.

Then, a third figure climbed down—a tall, burly man dressed in a Western-style suit of gray slacks, white shirt, casual sport coat and string tie. The man wore no Stetson on his salt-and-pepper head, but the sun's lingering rays glinted off the star badge pinned to his coat. The ranger's expression was stern. Bree's smile morphed into a scowl.

"What's the problem?" Brow furrowing, Cam shifted in his saddle.

"It's okay." Bree lifted one hand, palm out. "Well, it's not okay, but there's no physical threat. That's my boss, Captain Gaines."

Cam urged Rojo closer to her. "Come to haul you back to headquarters?"

"Try, anyway." She grimaced.

He let out a wry chuckle at her mulish tone. Bree shot him a glare. Swallowing another chuckle, Cam sucked his lips between his teeth and looked away.

The EMTs trotted over to the injured man, Gaines striding purposefully in their wake. Bree's loud sigh carried to Cam's ears despite the fading rumble whine of the helicopter rotors. She climbed down off her horse to meet her boss. Cam drifted Rojo closer to the pair so at least he might catch part of the conversation. Eavesdrop much? No, never. But he was making an exception to the rule today when so much lay at stake that affected him deeply.

"Bree, are you okay?" The man's voice was a smooth tenor wrapped in steel.

"I'm fine, Captain."

"Things can't go on this way." Gaines swept on, scarcely missing a beat for her response.

"I know it's been wild, sir, but—"

"You need to come back with me to Company C headquarters in Lubbock. We can't delay getting you into protection."

"What do you suggest, Captain? That I hole up at headquarters indefinitely? That's not practical."

"Not at headquarters, no, but I'm in discussion with the Marshals Service. Since you'll be testifying at several trials related to the issue that has you under threat with the Espinoza cartel, you would qualify for witness protection through the dates of the trials, followed by relocation."

"No." The single word cracked like a whip.

Gaines lifted a quieting hand. "I know it's not ideal, but it's your life we're considering here."

"Not ideal?" Bree's tone had gone up an octave. "Exactly, it's *my life*. You're asking me to leave my family and my career to become someone else. Not happening."

"But—"

She leaned closer to the captain, invading his personal space. "What are my recourses when the cartel finds me under my new identity?"

Gaines gave no ground as he shook his head. "The Marshals Service is exceptionally good at what they do. They don't lose people unless the subject does something stupid like willfully coming out of hiding or contacting someone from their old existence. And you're not that stupid. At least, I thought you weren't, but you've been testing my opinion of your judgment by refusing to come in."

"I'm on leave, and I have a job to do with those cattle." Bree waved at the herd.

The captain let out a low groan and rubbed his palm across his sharp chin. "You've been attacked twice in one day."

Cam mentally amended the tally to three times, but at least one of those times, the drone collision, might have been by accident. At any rate, he hoped so.

"Only once, sir—" Bree lifted her chin "—when I've had any reason to believe the attackers knew my identity. That was this morning. This afternoon, the three rustlers who accosted us, including Trout over there—" she gestured at the man the EMTs were loading onto a stretcher "—thought we were cowhands trying to stop them from taking the herd. This wasn't a personal attempt on my life. It was standard operating procedure for this gang of rustlers. The cartel does not know where I am right now. They *will* know as soon as I show up at headquarters."

Gaines let out an acquiescent grunt. "I'll grant you that the cartel probably has our office under surveillance, but they won't get to you there." He crossed his arms over his lean chest. "Be sensible. You're endangering yourself and others out here on your own."

Cam bent forward and rested his elbow on his saddle horn. "She's not on her own, sir."

The captain whirled toward him with a deep scowl. "And you are?"

"Cameron Wolfe, the Maguires' neighbor." He sat up tall in the saddle and met the fury with steady eyes. In a way, he didn't blame the ranger captain for his anger and frustration. The man was afraid for his colleague. But that didn't mean Cam needed to back down. "You're on my land at the moment. Bree and I are rounding up the herd that got stampeded during this morning's excitement. I've told her she doesn't need to feel obligated to do that, but apparently, she does."

Gaines narrowed his pale blue eyes. "You're the rancher who accosted Leon Waring and ended up helping fight off a sniper and taking down that attack helicopter."

"One and the same."

"Good work out there." The captain's expression relaxed marginally. "Now, will you please explain to your neighbor here that cooperating with law enforcement, not to mention her boss, is a wise idea?"

Cam chuckled. "I figure she's a sharp woman and can make her own choices."

The man's face reddened and his mouth opened as if to speak.

"No explaining necessary." Bree's brisk tone interrupted the exchange between Cam and her boss. "I am fully aware that I am in danger and that those I love are in danger, and even my work colleagues are in danger if I am in proximity to them. The cartel is not fussy about collateral damage and is not squeamish about using a person's family members to get close to their target. However, my disappearance into protection will not lessen the danger to my loved ones. If anything, that action will increase the risk, as the desperate hitters will be more prone to grab anyone available as leverage to flush me out. The only person who will be safer is me, and I can't put myself first in this situation."

Cam's heart swelled in appreciation of this woman's savvy and unselfish conclusions. If anyone got what she had so ably explained, he did. At one point in his own similar situation, he'd made the same decision she was making—to hold fast and stick it out, trusting for some other solution than uprooting his life. But then things happened and disappearing alone had become the only viable option. Now, Bree was in an uncannily similar position.

Cam jerked a decisive nod. "What she said."

Warmth cascaded through his insides at the naked gratitude in Bree's gaze upon him.

The captain's sour stare affected him not at all.

If only he could assure Bree this choice would turn out favorably for her, but her life hung precariously in the balance, and there was little anyone could do to affect the outcome but hope and pray. The cartel was coming for her, and things were likely to get messy. Cam would do anything in his power to ensure that any spilled blood was not hers, but the cartel had numbers and ruthlessness in its corner. God alone knew how long they could hold out against the overwhelming tide.

SEVEN

Weary and slumped in the saddle, Bree guided Teton to help push the last of the cattle through the gate into the home pasture near Cam's ranch headquarters. Just in time. Full dark spread across the prairie like spilled ink as the last sliver of the sun dipped below the distant mountain heights. Happily, a full moon and myriad twinkling stars studding the blue-black sky shed enough illumination to safely continue moving forward. The cattle picked up their pace, no doubt scenting the good water held in the spring-fed tank that had long been one of this ranch's richest features. Cam had done well to buy the place.

The injured animals trailed along last, but at least they continued onward. Except for the old pack mare and the lame gelding, who would be led to the barn, the other injured animals would have to wait until morning light to be lassoed and have their wounds treated. Tomorrow promised to be as busy as today, but hopefully without interruption by hostile forces.

She was relatively confident she'd spoken the truth to her captain when she'd claimed the cartel didn't currently know her whereabouts. On that premise, Captain Gaines had grumpily left without her in the medivac helicopter with the wounded prisoner. Of course, Dillon would need to be extra cautious going forward in case *sicarios* or cartel spies in the form of people or drones came sniffing around. She'd get in touch with her brother tonight, and they'd have that conversation.

"Let's head on up to the building site." Cam's voice pierced the darkness.

Bree turned her head toward the sound. His horse and rider silhouette stood out as a darker patch in the gloom. Behind him stood an additional pair of silhouettes, the wounded mare and lame gelding, she presumed.

"I'll be right behind you." She kneed Teton forward and took her gelding's reins from Cam, then followed him and his mare at an ambling walk in the direction of the looming barn.

They'd care for the animals they brought into the barn first and then go into the house and look after themselves. As grubby as she felt, a long, hot shower sounded like a major treat. Whether she'd eat something or simply call Dillon and then fall into bed afterward remained to be seen.

"My stomach is eating my backbone," Cam said as if sensing her thoughts about food.

Bree chuckled, the sound tired and faint on the breeze. "My eyelids need propping up. Do you have any toothpicks?"

Cam's laugh warmed her heart. Something about coming in off the range in this man's company felt so right that it was scary. She'd have to watch her wayward emotions and rein them in severely. A life crisis was no sane time to be entertaining romantic notions.

Forty-five minutes later, the horses fed, watered, and injuries tended, Bree and Cam entered through the side door of the Diamond-W's two-story home, a sturdy but plain dwelling that was significantly smaller than the Double-Bar-D's sprawling single-story house. The entrance led into a small mudroom where they hung their hats on pegs and washed up in the scrub sink. Then Cam led the way into a neatly laid out but compact kitchen redolent with the smells of Mexican spices and tortillas. A squat, round woman in a flour-coated apron stood near the stove.

The middle-aged cook grinned at them, brown eyes twinkling. "It is a good thing I heard those cattle bawling from a mile away, so I knew when to put the tamales in the oven. They are almost ready."

"Thanks, Estrella. You're a gem. Did Luis make it back from checking the irrigation lines?"

"Yes, Señor Cam. All was well with the pipelines. He is in the work shed mending a bridle."

Bree appreciated that Cam properly pronounced his hand's Hispanic name as *Lwees*. The knowledge suggested native Southwestern roots, which gave her a hint about Cam's origins. Or maybe it only meant he'd been polite enough to pick up on the pronunciation when he'd first met his ranch help.

Bree responded appropriately as Cam quickly made the introductions between the women, and then he glanced deeper into the house. "Do we have time for quick showers before we eat?"

The older woman waved them away. "The food will be on the table when you return."

Bree followed her host up a set of slightly creaky, original hardwood stairs to a guest bedroom furnished and decorated in a country theme. With a grateful sigh, she lowered her saddlebags onto the padded bench at the foot of the bed. Cam's gray eyes studied her solemnly, and she all but heard his unvoiced pledge: *No one will get to you here.* She met the look straight-on. Her heart fluttered and her stomach did a silly pirouette.

"The bathroom is at the end of the hall." He

jerked a thumb in that direction. "I'll be down-stairs in the master. The Franklins upgraded it to include an en suite. We can meet in the kitchen. Estrella's tamales are the best I've ever had."

His slight smirk communicated that he was well acquainted with her fatigue and sympa-thized, but an authentic Mexican dinner was not to be missed.

"I'll be there." She nodded.

He withdrew, and his boots thump-creaked down the stairs. Releasing a long breath, Bree opened one side of her bags and drew out a change of clothing—just a T-shirt and a pair of soft leggings—plus a few toiletries she'd packed in anticipation of a possible night on the range. Sleeping in a house in a bed beat the bare ground in a tent by a mile, but a part of her prickled with unease that perhaps she'd be bringing danger to Cam and his innocent housekeeper and ranch hand. But that risk would be real anywhere she went. For the moment, her neighbor's house was as safe as anywhere else.

The shower was as wonderful as she'd antic-ipated it to be. When she arrived downstairs, clean and in comfortable attire, Cam was already in the dining room, where Estrella was arranging the food on the table. From what Bree caught of the conversation he was having with his house-keeper, he had been updating her on their eventful day on the range. The woman was properly appalled and kept flapping her apron and making sympathetic sounds. Then, at Bree's appearance, she smacked plump hands together.

"Sit, sit." The woman waved Bree to a vacant seat. "You must be starving."

With a nod toward Cam, Bree obeyed the housekeeper and bowed her head with them both while her host spoke a simple table prayer. They dug in, and the meal was beyond scrumptious. Bree made sure to express her appreciation to Estrella, who remained with them, sometimes sitting, and sometimes fetching this and that, including a plate of flavorful cinnamon churros for dessert. She did not eat, claiming she and her husband, Luis, had eaten earlier. The housekeeper and Cam made pleasant and relaxed company, but Bree was under no illusion that she, with her drooping eyelids, was any kind of company at all.

As she shoveled the last yummy bite into her mouth, she caught Cam eyeing her speculatively. "What?" She narrowed her gaze at him.

"Sorry." He shook his head. "I was just thinking that maybe Estrella could be persuaded to even out that accidental haircut you received this morning." He ended the sentence with a grimace, clearly recalling the events surrounding that sniper bullet.

Bree caught her breath. "You're right. I need

the damage fixed. I've always had long hair. This does feel…strange." She ran her hands through her ragged ends.

"No offense intended. The short style suits you."

"Indeed, it does." Estrella clicked her tongue. "Of course, I will be happy to provide a trim, but in the morning. You look ready to fall asleep on your plate."

The woman let out a hearty laugh that buoyed Bree's spirits. She may have lost a chunk of her hair, but she hadn't lost her life.

"Let me help you with the dishes first." She rose from the table.

"Nonsense, *mi querido*. It is my pleasure to serve such a brave one. Go get some well-deserved rest."

Estrella grabbed a pile of plates and bustled from the room. Cam seconded his housekeeper's urging. Gratefully, Bree trudged up the stairs, flopped into the bed and promptly fell into a deep slumber.

Bree had no idea how long she had slept when a firm hand on her shoulder shook her into startled awareness. Sitting up with a cry, her fist flew at her assailant and smacked a fleshy target. Pain jolted through her fist and up her arm. The shadowed figure at her bedside staggered backward with a deep *whoof.* Bree fought free of her bedcovers and leaped to the floor in full Krav Maga mode.

"Bree!" Cam's powerful rumble halted an instinctive kick before it left the ground.

The last of the sleep thrall fell away from her senses. "Cam? What are you doing rousting me like this? It's still dark out." Her sideways glance at the cracks between the curtains on the window revealed blackness outside.

Cam huffed, a switch clicked, and the overhead light sprang on. Bree blinked at her tall, pajama-clad host, his expression etched in taut planes. The paleness of his thin facial scar stood out against a red splotch where she'd struck him. There would be a bruise.

Bree's hand went to her mouth. "I'm so sorry." Her warm breath feathered against her fingers.

"No matter. Considering the situation you're in, I shouldn't have startled you." His words came out gruff, some deep emotion shading his eyes—not related to being sucker-punched.

Bree's gut seized. "What is it?"

"There's a fire at your ranch. It's visible from here."

"No, no, no!" Heart trip hammering, she raced to the window and threw the curtains aside.

Her mouth went stone dry. It was true. A red-gold stain on the landscape pulsed on the distant horizon. The fire must be substantial to stand out so visibly. Her stomach wrung like a dishrag.

"Dillon." His name emerged in a strangled tone. She could hardly speak for the constriction of her throat. "I have to go."

Bree whirled toward the exit and slammed against a large body adamant to obstruct her way. Sturdy arms wrapped her close, but she fought. If she could get her arms free of Cam's python grip, she'd punch him again.

"Whoa, whoa, whoa!" Cam clutched Bree close despite the sharp kick she landed on his shin, sending pain splintering up his leg. Another bruise for sure. "You didn't let me finish. Dillon's okay. Everyone at your ranch is all right."

She went still as if frozen in place. "What? How do you know?"

"He called me."

Bree went limp, and Cam hazarded releasing her but kept a grip on her shoulders in case she crumpled from the sudden relief. He didn't dare give a second thought to how good and right this woman felt in his arms. Painful kick not withstanding.

She glared up at him. "He called *you*. Why didn't he call me?"

"He knew you'd be furious if you weren't told

right away, but he wanted me to stop you from doing exactly what you were trying to do—rush to the scene."

Her eyes flicked from right to left, thoughts clearly churning. "Because the whole purpose of the fire is to draw me out. This was arson."

"Dillon thinks so, though they won't know for sure until the blaze is out. The fire department is there already."

Bree's gaze hardened on him. "What is burning?"

"Your machine shed. The fuel inside the building is causing the blaze to be exceptionally intense."

"Not the house, or the barn, or the bunkhouse?"

Cam's blood chilled. If any of those structures had been set on fire, people and livestock would have been at risk. Not that the cartel would care. This scenario involving only the machine shed showed uncharacteristic restraint.

Bree pulled away from him, hugging herself and pacing. "The arsonist must be a local, not a ruthless *sicario*. Someone after the bounty, but a person with rural roots who would despise injuring animals and prefers not to hurt untargeted people."

"I had about reached that conclusion myself."

She stopped her restless movement and fixed a steady stare on him beneath raised eyebrows.

"I would surmise the two rustlers who got away out at the playa as the culprits, except the rustler gang that's been operating around here has the same respect for life as the cartel, which is none. Do I have to start suspecting friends and neighbors now?"

Cam's heart sank. She'd asked a legitimate question—the sort of agonizing idea he'd dismissed to his sorrow at an earlier point in his life. *Please, God, don't let this situation turn out for her the same way it did for me.*

He drew in a deep breath and let it out slowly. "A lot of people are struggling financially, and the bounty is substantial. Desperation makes people vulnerable to temptation. But then, we don't want to jump to conclusions. There could be another explanation."

Bree side-eyed him like she knew he was attempting to soften a bitter blow. "If you think of one, please let me know."

Cam puffed out a dry chuckle. "I'll be sure to do that. But on the bright side, since you didn't come running when the smoke signal went up, anyone on the bounty hunt might decide you're nowhere in the area. The net could widen, taking some of the focus off the immediate area."

"A little breathing room, maybe?" She stopped pacing and faced him, hands on hips. Her green eyes lit with a glimmer of hope.

Cam forced a smile to his lips. Any reprieve would be temporary, but they'd take what they could get. "Lay low here on the Diamond-W like it's your safe house on the open range, and let's see what happens."

Her eyes narrowed. "I hate this."

The vehemence of her tone resonated within him, and he nodded. "I know. I hate it *for* you. In the morning, we can figure out clandestine means to contact your brother and your captain."

"Morning? Isn't it that already? It may still be dark, but it must be after midnight."

Cam snorted. "Technically, 2:00 a.m. counts as a new day, but I'm still all for a few more hours of rack time before the fresh workday starts."

Bree's shoulders drooped. "I don't know if I'll be able to get back to sleep."

"Give it a try. There's always milk that can be warmed down in the kitchen, but Estrella is likely to show up as soon as there's a stir in the kitchen. She'll hover like a mother goose. She and Luis have a small suite attached to the back of the house adjoining her culinary domain, and I know from the experience of trying to sneak out of the house early that she sleeps lightly."

A meager smile brightened the dark expression on Bree's face. "I think I'll crawl back under the covers and try to get my heart rate under control. I'm sorry, by the way."

"For what?"

She tapped her cheek on the location where she had struck him. Cam touched the spot on his face and found a little heat and swelling. He'd have a bruise by the time he woke to start the day.

He grinned at her. "You pack a wallop, ma'am. Remind me not to get in the way of your fist again."

Bree let out an unladylike snort, and Cam turned to go with a small wave. "Sleep tight."

"And fast. I'll be up by sunrise. I don't believe in burning daylight. We've got critters to look after."

He knocked lightly on the doorframe and awarded her a grin. "I'll meet you downstairs for breakfast at six sharp."

"You got it." She answered his grin with her own. "Don't be late."

"As if." He snorted and headed for the stairway, chuckling.

Who would have believed that tense encounter would end on a positive note? Cam's heart hurt for Dillon over the loss of property. What a mess, creating all sorts of headaches. But everyone was still upright and breathing. They'd have to take small mercies where they could get them.

He returned to his Southwestern-themed bedroom and tucked himself under the covers he had so suddenly vacated. Bree thought she might have trouble getting to sleep again. She wasn't the only one.

Cam closed his eyes, and his last glimpse of Bree, flaming hair disheveled from sleep and green eyes gleaming as if determination alone would prevail against all threats, appeared mirrored against his eyelids. Stubborn. Unconventionally beautiful. Resourceful and undeniably courageous. Those were a few of the descriptors he'd apply to Brianna Maguire. His dainty socialite former fiancée had been this woman's polar opposite, but she'd been the sort of shiny woman the man Cam used to be had thought he wanted. But that was then. His eyes had been rudely opened since.

If he was honest with himself, dealing with Bree's straightforward manner was like a breath of fresh air compared to the demands and expectations Tessa had possessed, envisioning herself as the first lady of a Western ranch empire. Discovering Cam had no desire to play cattle baron—that ranch life meant she would work alongside everyone else—had done as much to end the relationship as her contempt for his resurgence of faith in Jesus Christ. In the end, she'd betrayed him in the worst way possible. Cam's heart wrung at the memory, but the misery had dulled to the ache of a bruise rather than a deep knife cut.

At the time, he hadn't known if he could survive the pain, especially when her betrayal took a back seat to the other... The cruel knowledge he scarcely dared allow himself to think about. Almost worse than anything the cartel could dish out. Yet here he was—alive but hiding in plain sight. Forevermore not the man he used to be, and perhaps the better for it...if he could ever stop looking over his shoulder for the enemy coming after him.

What a pair he and Bree made. Both of them fugitives, not from the law but from the very criminals who should be locked up. Life could scarcely get more ironic than that. What tomorrow might bring, God alone knew. If the Espinoza cartel had its way, Bree's life would end in bullets and blood. Cam couldn't let them succeed if he hoped to continue living with himself.

But how could he stop the cartel? He had no idea. If only helplessness and despair didn't mock him like dark pits eager to swallow him whole.

EIGHT

Bree leaned her folded arms on the top bar of a corral fence, her gaze riveted on the tall figure working with a lovely bay filly. Cam had informed her that he recently purchased the two-year-old for breeding stock, and someone had delivered the animal to the ranch only three days ago. Her neighbor knew his way around horse training, that was for sure. The young animal trotted obediently in a circle around him, where he stood in the center of the corral, holding a rope attached to the horse's halter in one hand and a training stick in the other. The pricked-forward ears and slight angle of the equine head toward Cam indicated the trainer had captured the filly's attention. At a cluck from Cam's tongue and a flick of the stick with a small flag on its end, the horse picked up its pace to a slow lope.

Dust from flying hooves tickled Bree's nostrils and she stifled a sneeze but did not curb the smile that spread across her lips. This was a good life. Fresh air. Honest toil. The sun kissing her skin. Congenial company like the man who captured her attention more than the fine horse he trained. It hardly seemed possible that danger lurked like a predator sniffing at the perimeter of her life. Waiting. Watching. Ready to pounce.

The smile dimmed as she yanked her thoughts away from the dark precipice. Had it really been a whole two weeks since the fire at her place? Bree had kept in touch with her brother, not using her phone, which might be tracked, but Cam's. Dillon was already preparing to rebuild the machine shed, and orders were in to replace the ruined equipment. The destruction was a big-time, resource-stealing annoyance on a working ranch, but no living creature had been hurt. The fire had been officially declared arson, but nobody was yet in custody for the crime. Bree was waiting to hear back from her captain about a lead the rangers were pursuing.

Her heart wrung with an unvoiced plea that the culprit not be someone she knew. It was bad enough to have to suspect every stranger who came through the area without feeling unsafe around friends and neighbors. Not that she'd been out and about so far, but she couldn't pretend the world wasn't waiting for her to rejoin it. Something that probably needed to happen soon.

This idyll here at Cam's ranch had seemed

to stretch on forever. Like she'd found safety that would last. Her heart willed the reprieve to go on forever, but her head knew better. Officially, she was using vacation days she had accumulated, and Captain Gaines was continuing to work with the Marshals Service to arrange the dreaded witness protection. Unofficially, she was hiding in plain sight, but realistically, this time on the Diamond-W could only be the proverbial calm before the storm.

With every passing minute, she potentially brought danger to the courageous man and his kind hired help who had taken her in. They—no, *she* needed a plan for when the cartel found her. The thought of leaving everyone and everything to adopt a new identity nauseated her. But what were her alternatives?

Bree had yet to find one, and there had to be a limit to how much longer she involved Cam. Too bad she was reluctant to admit the threshold was upon them and make the break. She was getting too comfortable here.

Bree dropped her arms to her sides and stepped back from the corral. Maybe she should—

"Whoa!" Cam spoke to the colt and brought the animal to a stop.

Bree also froze, gaze fixed on the training scene. The filly turned its nose to Cam and walked docilely, head low and calm, toward his still figure. Cam crooned to the animal and rubbed a hand between its doe eyes. Bree's skin tingled pleasantly as if she were the creature receiving the gentle touch.

Get a grip, Maguire! Bree shook herself and let out a huff that echoed a loud whiffle from the filly now following Cam to the barn.

"Let me brush her down," Bree called, and Cam acknowledged her request with a smile over his shoulder and a wave.

She joined Cam in the dim barn that smelled pleasantly of fresh hay, grabbed a horse brush, and got busy on the filly's sleek but slightly sweaty hide.

Cam patted the horse's rump. "She's coming along nicely, if I do say so myself."

"Agreed. You're a good horse trainer."

"Competent." He shrugged. "Hardly an expert."

The crackle hum of vehicle tires on gravel interrupted their conversation and brought both their heads around toward the ranch yard.

A muscle tightened in Cam's jaw, and Bree's gut twisted. She took a step away from the horse, but Cam raised a forestalling hand. "Stay here out of sight. I'll go see who it is and what they want."

Bree bottled a low growl in her throat. "I hate—" she started, but he was already striding from the barn before she could finish telling him how much she despised being on edge all the time and him being in danger because of her. Not that the observation was new information, but revulsion for the situation had pushed the words out of her mouth.

Laying the brush aside and leaving the filly tied in the alleyway between the stalls, Bree drew the pistol from her appendix carry and crept up to the open door. She didn't have to show herself to listen to whatever conversation Cam conducted with their uninvited guests. Quite probably, the visit was benign, but Bree was hardly going to rely on that possibility, especially when the intruding vehicle seemed to be coming up the driveway entirely too fast.

Remaining in the shadows, Bree put her eye to a crack between the door and the casing. A dark blue SUV with blacked-out windows skidded to a stop with a ping of gravel against the undercarriage mere yards from Cam's stalwart figure. He stood with legs set apart, offering a solid balance base for any necessary action. One hand subtly hovered near his own pistol in the holster on his hip. As he'd consistently proved, the man was no stranger to defending against aggression.

Taut silence fell over the yard. The late-morning heat baked the bare earth with a near-audible sizzle. Or maybe the sizzle was Bree's nerves strung tight as electrified fence wire.

At last, the driver's-side window rolled down and a man's hand reached out, showing a placating palm. A pleasant, round face appeared behind the friendly hand.

"Hola, señor." The man grinned, but the toothy facial expression sent a shiver down Bree's spine.

Maybe the guy was here for an innocent purpose, and she was overreacting, but she didn't think so. Smarmy is as smarmy does, and that too-big grin rang false, which led to expectations of deceptive behavior. Too bad she wasn't close enough to read the guy's eyes, but at least Cam was, and she trusted him. The visible stiffening of his spine didn't bode well.

"Stranger, whatever you're selling, I'm not in the market for it." Cam's tone brooked no nonsense.

"No, no, you misunderstand," the man in the car protested, starting to open his door. "Let me show—"

"Stay right there." The barked words and the big hand on a pistol butt stopped the stranger midmotion and midsentence. "I don't know you, and I didn't invite you. If you're some innocent passer-by who's lost his way out in the boonies, my apologies. Go on back to the county road and turn left. Continue in that direction for five miles and you'll reach a state highway that will take you to Interstate 27. Road signs will show how to get to Lubbock or Amarillo or whatever way you want to go from there."

The stranger's smile disappeared into a sneer. "I am not lost, and I do not need directions. You are not a very friendly man, *señor.* I might become offended at your lack of hospitality."

"Offending you is the least of my concerns. I've been hearing rumors about cartel hitmen rampaging around the countryside. In fact, my neighbor recently lost his machine shed to arson, so forgive me if I'm a mite protective of my property. Unless you can convince me that you have legitimate business, you'd better turn your vehicle around and vamoose."

The stranger's face turned deep red, and Bree's heart began hammering against her ribs. Violence hung like gunpowder in the air. All it would take is a spark to turn explosive.

Behind Bree, the filly let out a shrill whinny and slammed her hoof against the floor. Even as Bree whirled on whatever threat crept toward her back, she dropped into a low crouch. A shadowed figure rushed at her, and the shotgun in his hands boomed.

At the shotgun's blast Cam involuntarily swiveled toward the sound. But his peripheral vision caught sudden movement from the man in the car. He forced himself to whirl back toward the immediate threat. Bree could take care of herself, couldn't she? *Please, God, make it so.*

Cam yanked his pistol from its holster as the snarling stranger lunged from his vehicle, bringing an automatic weapon to bear on him. Cam's gun spat milliseconds before the stranger's. The man grunted and staggered, throwing his aim off, and the burst of bullets from the automatic missed Cam. But not by much. The hiss of speeding lead nipped his ear. Cam pulled the trigger again, and his assailant collapsed. He rushed forward and kicked the man's weapon away even as another blast echoed from the barn.

Not a shotgun.

A pistol.

Bree.

A weight the size of an elephant left Cam's chest. She was alive and fighting back.

He had to help her. There was no time to address the injuries of the man from the car, who lay still, eyes closed, bleeding from his head and chest but breathing. Cam rushed for the barn but stopped himself from plunging willy-nilly into the dimness where grunts and smacks betrayed an ongoing struggle. At least the shooting had stopped.

Pulse throbbing in his neck, Cam pressed his

back against the outside wall and peered around the edge of the door. Bree's pistol lay on the floor. Nearby, she and a wiry man struggled for control of a shotgun. The man was getting a taste of her booted feet and sharp elbows.

Cam stepped through the doorway with a shout. "Drop the gun!"

Wisely, Bree leaped away from her assailant to give Cam a clear shot at the guy. Not so wisely, the man attempted to bring his weapon to bear on her, and Cam pulled the trigger. The attacker yelped, dropped his gun—finally—and clutched his wounded arm. A high, keening sound came from his throat.

Bree snatched up the pistol and the shotgun then spared Cam a nod. "Thanks. Are you…all right?" Her words came out with a wheeze, like she was struggling to catch her breath.

"Not a scratch. You?" He scanned her figure from top to bottom and spotted no obvious wounds.

"He took a shot at me, and I took a shot at him, but then we were too close to each other. After he knocked the pistol from my hand, I took a shotgun stock to the solar plexus. No bullets, thankfully. But not for lack of trying." She nodded at the door swinging on its hinges behind him.

Cam spared a glance over his shoulder and found the wooden door pock-marked with lethal pellets at about chest and head height. His blood ran cold at the thought of the consequences if the blast had struck her.

"Looks like the guy in the car came in as a distraction so this hombre could sneak up on you." He waggled his gun at the scowling shotgun-wielder.

"Yep. This was planned." She shook her head. "Apparently, I've been located."

"You should have let me kill you." The wounded prisoner sneered. "You have no idea what's coming for you. There are many of us and only two of you."

"Nonsense." Bree snorted, seemingly breathing easier but rubbing her breastbone. "When you come after one of us, you take on the entire law enforcement apparatus of the great State of Texas."

"Are you certain they will be enough? They are not with you today."

Cam ground his teeth at the sly expression on the criminal's face. "Enough talk out of you. Move." He stepped aside from the door and waved for the man to walk ahead of him out of the barn. "You'll get your taste of Texas law enforcement hospitality all right."

"What he said." Bree stepped up alongside Cam, her face pale but her eyes blazing like sunstruck emeralds.

Side by side, they followed the prisoner out into the sunshine. A sturdy figure in a brightly colored skirt and white blouse rushed at them from the direction of the house. Estrella had a rifle clutched in her hands, but she kept the muzzle pointed skyward as she came toward them.

"What has happened, *señor*?" The housekeeper slowed as she neared, and then she stopped, pressing a fist to her mouth as her gaze swept over the incapacitated bad guys. Estrella huffed, scowled, and then shook her head. "I will call the sheriff and emergency services." Turning on her heel, the woman scurried back to the house in a swirl of skirts.

"Thank you," Cam called after her.

Bree pulled zip ties from her pockets and secured the wrists of her attacker. Droplets of red stained the ground from his arm wound, and he let out a pained grunt as she tightened the binding. Red-faced fury had replaced the pallor of shock on her face, so Cam inferred she wasn't inclined to spare the guy much sympathy. But she did order him to sit down on a nearby hay bale before he fell over.

As he sullenly complied, she grabbed a nearby length of rope and began to bind it around his arm as a temporary tourniquet. Not so devoid of sympathy, after all, or perhaps simply practical about preserving human life, as well as a potential witness to testify that his boss, Alonzo Espinoza, had ordered him to kill Bree. Not that such testimony was likely. Cartel muscle was usually more afraid of their ruthless master than what the US legal system could do to them.

Bree had her would-be killer under control, so Cam allowed himself to take his eyes off her and squat down by the man from the car. The *sicario* had taken a bullet to his upper chest and one had grazed the side of his head, knocking him out. Neither wound bled any longer because the cartel hitman was no longer breathing and the heart had stopped pumping. Cam frowned and heaved out a long breath.

It wasn't the first time Cam had been forced to take a life, but he'd hoped the last time was going to *be* the last time. Now this. But trouble had come looking for *him*, not the other way around, and he'd learned the hard way to respond with appropriate force. Hesitation got you, a colleague, or a bystander, dead. This time, it could have been Bree who might have paid the ultimate price if he hadn't made this guy pay it instead.

"What now?" Bree said from behind him.

Cam grunted and rose to face her. "This one didn't make it."

"I see that." She nodded solemnly. "Thank you. But that's not what I meant. What do I do now? I mean, I know I need to leave here. I've stayed too long." She looked away and pressed her lips together to constrain whatever railing outcry against her situation was striving to leave her throat.

"I know a place we can go."

Bree shook her head emphatically. "Not we. Me."

"I don't think the cartel is going to be happy about my interference. I'll have to lay low, too. We might as well do it together."

A slight glint of humor entered her eyes. "Methinks the Knight of the Range has dubbed himself this ranger's protector. As much as I appreciate the sentiment, I don't think the cartel will bother you if you're not harboring me. How are they even going to find out you killed one of their own? This one can't talk and the other guy—" she gestured to the desperado slumped on the hay bale "—will be in custody."

Cam sent Bree a bleak smile. "Trust me. They'll find out."

The vast intelligence network cartels worked hard to achieve, reaching into law enforcement itself, was another lesson Cam had learned the hard way.

The crunch of feet across gravel drew their attention. Estrella hurried up to them, clutching Cam's phone that he'd left in the house while he'd trained the filly. He reached out for the cell, but his housekeeper bypassed him in favor of Bree.

"It is for you, *señorita*. Your boss."

Bree released an audible sigh and took the phone. Cam eyed her with raised brows. What now?

Their understanding with her division was that anyone needing to contact her would do so through Cam's phone so that she would not have to activate her own and risk being tracked. Estrella had been made aware of this arrangement, and Cam had given her permission to answer his cell if he was not there to do so.

"When I tell him what just happened," Bree said, "the captain will no doubt want to connect with us both and get initial statements." Sidling closer to Cam, she tapped the screen and activated the speaker.

Cam appreciated the inclusion, but his gut tightened in anticipation of what Captain Gaines might say.

"The woman who answered my call said you just survived a cartel assault." The captain's words came out high-pitched and staccato as if pressure were being applied to his vocal cords.

"That's correct," Bree said. "The sheriff and emergency services are on the way. We have one wounded *sicario*, and the other—well, he won't need a doctor."

Her boss hissed in a breath. Glass suddenly shattered in the background, and someone shouted.

The hair on the back of Cam's neck stood on end. "What's going on there?"

"Headquarters has been under attack for the past ten minutes."

Cam's body went rigid. That was the farthest thing from what he'd figured on hearing, but it did explain the extreme tension in Gaines's voice.

"What do you mean?" Bree's tone was shrill.

"Cartel presence has been thick around headquarters for the past week. We knew they were hanging around to intercept you if you came in, but none of the suspicious characters was doing anything we could arrest them for. But now, all of a sudden, we've got sharpshooters in nearby taller buildings plinking the bullet-resistant glass in our windows with armor-piercing rounds."

All color ebbed from Bree's face and she swayed. Cam caught her arm, steadying her.

"Casualties?" Cam asked.

"Two wounded from shrapnel. We're all taking cover, but—" Somewhere nearby, more glass exploded, and Gaines spat an angry word.

"I'll be there as fast as I can." Bree pulled away from Cam, her expression setting like steel.

"Don't you dare come here," Gaines bellowed. "That's an order. Secure yourself somehow until the Marshals Service contacts you to enter WIT-SEC. Should only be a day or two. We're done playing wait and hope for the best." Glass shattered again, and the captain cried out. "This can't be happening. We're the law! They're—"

A loud thump sounded, like something falling, and then the call went dead.

The wounded *sicario* sitting on the hay bale began to chuckle. A sinister solo in the stunned silence.

NINE

The phone slipped from Bree's sweat-slick fist. Cam's hand moved in a blur and caught it even as his fierce gaze seized hers. She straightened her spine.

"You heard the captain." She nodded toward him. "Time to hole up somewhere for a few days. You said you know a place?"

"I do, but I'll tell you about it later." He jerked his head at their prisoner.

Bree glared at the *sicario*, whose gaze met hers. The man's black eyes glittered like wet stones, and his lips seemed set in a permanent sneer. No doubt his ears were perked to overhear anything he could about their plans. All the cartel would have to do was send in a lawyer to talk to the prisoner, and the lawyer would get the information to pass along to Alonzo Espinoza.

Engine noises began to grow from the direction of the county road. Minutes later, a sheriff's vehicle pulled into the yard, followed closely by an ambulance. The next half hour passed in a flurry of activity as the wounded outlaw received first aid. Both desperados were placed into the ambulance; one strapped to a gurney and handcuffed to the railing, the other in a body bag.

The lanky sheriff's deputy frowned at the proceedings even as he took Bree's and Cam's statements. Estrella also served as a witness. She hadn't seen much of what had gone on, but she'd heard things that corroborated the sequence of events.

Bree stood nearby, shifting her weight from foot to foot, as the deputy wrapped up the interview. At last, he put his recorder away and settled his gaze on Bree.

"Too much excitement around these parts." His tone bordered on the accusing.

Standing at Bree's side, Cam let out a wordless snarl. "You can't blame a fellow law enforcement officer for doing her job. It's the cartel who has taken this vendetta to a surreal level. But then, Alonzo Espinoza hasn't been quite rational since his daughter was kidnapped by the Ortega cartel. He got her back by a fluke of happenstance, but now he goes over the edge if anyone messes with his family."

Bree whipped her gaze up at him. How did Cameron Wolfe know unreleased details about

Espinoza and the notorious incident in New Mexico? The kidnapping and recovery of Espinoza's daughter, who was being trafficked by the Ortega cartel, had been kept under wraps. All the media had known was that the border patrol and DEA had wrapped up an Ortega trafficking ring with backslaps all the way around.

Then again, Cam had confessed he'd been involved in something with the DEA that had wound up costing him his relationship with his fiancée. Questions for her new neighbor piled up behind her lips, but now was not the time to ask them. Her narrow-eyed gaze on him promised a later discussion, and his slight nod and heightened color indicated he'd received the message.

Bree turned back to face the deputy. "Have you heard anything about what's happening at ranger headquarters in Lubbock?"

The man frowned. "What a mess." He shook his head, not in negation but in what Bree interpreted as amazed disgust. "Heard on the radio that the building got shot to smithereens, but I guess it's over now. Ended as quickly as it started. The cartel soldiers withdrew as suddenly as they attacked. Only minutes before the Lubbock Police Department SWAT team showed up loaded for bear."

"Casualties?" Cam asked the question on the tip of Bree's tongue.

She held her breath for the answer.

The deputy sighed. "Last I heard, there were a bunch of minor injuries from flying glass, but no one in the building took a bullet."

Bree breathed out a long sigh. "I'm so thankful."

"Amen," said Cam and the deputy in chorus.

"I'll get along then." The latter looked from Bree to Cam and back again. "What are your plans?"

Cam's lips flattened into a grim smile. "Let's just say we've got one and leave it at that."

The deputy shrugged and got into his sheriff's department SUV. Bree's eyes followed the dust of the retreating vehicle until the haze dissipated in the heavy air.

Then she turned to Cam with a pointed look. "What next, *caballero*?"

"Let's saddle up." Cam's tone was gruff, and he didn't meet her stare or respond to her designation of him as a mounted warrior. Without another word, he whirled and headed for the barn.

Bree followed on his heels. No conversation passed between them as they prepared their horses for a journey cross-country to where she didn't yet know. That she was content not to ask until they left the ranch spoke volumes about the level of trust she'd developed toward Cam Wolfe. And yet, nagging questions remained.

Teeth on edge, Bree gave a last jerk, tightening her saddle cinch.

Estrella hustled into the barn, arms laden with packages. "I have brought you food and supplies for your journey that will last many days."

"You're a gem." Smiling, Cam accepted the packages from her and began fitting them into panniers on the packsaddle. "I'm relying on you and Luis to look after everything while we're gone."

"You may depend upon us."

"I do—too much so, lately. We can talk about a raise for both of you when I return."

"Sí, señor." Estrella's countenance brightened.

Five minutes later, Bree on Teton trailed Cam on Rojo, with the pack mare—not the injured Myra, but an animal that had been delivered to the ranch along with the new filly—ambling behind on a lead rope. They headed in a south-westerly direction.

"Okay, spill," she said. "Where are we headed?"

"The Diamond-W has a line shack on the backside of nowhere." He turned in the saddle as she trotted Teton up beside him. "I found it when I inspected the property prior to purchasing it. Used to be a place for cowpokes to stay when they were rounding up strays far from the home place, but the cabin didn't look like it had been used in years. The conditions will be primitive. Plus, we may have to cold camp so no one on land or in the air spots smoke coming from the chimney."

Bree jerked a nod. "Do you think a little discomfort intimidates me at this point?" She bit her lower lip against blurting out more in the same sarcastic vein.

She hadn't intended her tone to be so snarky—not toward *him* anyway—but she was beyond angry, thoroughly frustrated, and, yes, quite a bit scared. If Alonzo Espinoza was willing to mount an attack against a law enforcement headquarters on United States' soil, there were no lengths to which he wouldn't go to get her. She'd thought she understood that, but the unprovoked assault in Lubbock brought the truth home to her. Those were her colleagues, her friends, who had been under attack.

At least the siege had been short-lived when other law enforcement agencies had mobilized to aid the rangers. No such rapid response would be coming for Cam and her out on the open range.

He reached over and squeezed her shoulder. The warm, steady touch melted a thin layer of the ice block that had taken up residence in her core. Unless something drastic happened to change her situation, soon she would be saying *adiós* to everything and everyone she'd ever known. Bree's heart tore. How could she go on?

* * *

Beneath Cam's palm, the rock that was Bree's shoulder abruptly melted into a slump. How hopeless she must feel. Cam's gut twisted. If anyone understood what was going on inside her, it was him. Telling his own complete story to her couldn't wait much longer, and she might be the only person on the planet to whom he'd feel safe telling it. But first, they needed to get to somewhere relatively safe and out of sight.

Next to him, Bree suddenly hauled back on her horse's reins and stopped. Cam pulled Rojo to a halt and turned the stallion to face her.

Her brows pinched together and faint lines between them formed a *V* on her forehead. "I understand about not lighting the fireplace in the shack, but what will we do with our horses? Their presence will give away our location to anyone scouting the area, especially by air."

"Good question." He offered her a smile that hopefully might relieve some tension. Then again, probably not. Nothing in this situation contributed to relaxation. "The shack stands near a spring-fed stream, and the grass is plentiful. We'll hide our tack in the lean-to attached to the cabin and set the horses free like they're simply loose and grazing a natural pasture. And because it *is* a natural pasture with more arid ground farther away, the animals are almost certain to stick around close by if we need them."

Bree offered a meager nod. "It's not a guarantee they won't wander off, like staking them out on ropes or keeping them in a corral, but I agree with the likelihood of them staying close by. If we're attacked, we may not be able to get to them as quickly as we would like, but in this situation, the emphasis is more on hiding than escaping—at least once we're at the cabin."

"Agreed. To complete the camouflage, we can push any cattle we run across over into that pasture as well. Then it will thoroughly appear to be assorted livestock loose on the range, a natural occurrence on a ranch."

A smirk appeared on Bree's lips and the tension lines on her face smoothed. "You think of everything, Mr. Wolfe. One would think dodging bad guys was a way of life for you."

Cam's jaw dropped, a protest forming on his tongue, but he halted the disclaimer before it emerged in words. Deflection of such remarks had become a reflex with him for self-preservation, but he didn't need that tactic with this woman. What would she think of him when she heard the full truth? He suppressed a shudder and forced a chuckle that came out more like a hiss of steam than an expression of wry humor.

With a narrow-eyed look, Bree bumped her

horse's ribs with her boot heels, and Teton moved out obediently. Cam shut his mouth and brought Rojo around beside her. Silence fell, except for the muted thud of hooves against packed earth and the chuff of horses breathing easy. Scents of sage and juniper wafted on a welcome breeze that did its bit to relieve the relentless heat of the sun.

"I need to call Dillon," Bree suddenly exclaimed . "I can't believe my mind has been in such knots that I haven't thought about him. The way the gossip grapevine works around here, he'll soon know about the incident at your place…if he doesn't already."

She swiveled at the waist and pulled the sat phone from her saddle bag. They'd both left their cells at Cam's ranch since they were the devices most susceptible to tracking. It was unlikely even the cartel's considerable resources stretched to the ability to locate a particular satellite phone.

Bree barely had the sat phone in her hand when it rang. She gasped, and the instrument slipped. Cam reached out and caught it. He could hardly blame her for being skittish.

"Let me answer," he said.

She shrugged but didn't speak. Her face had gone so pale the dusting of freckles stood out on her high cheekbones. No doubt, dreading what fresh bad news might be coming this time, recent phone calls having brought nothing good.

Cam pressed the talk button. "This is Cameron Wolfe. Speak."

Heavy breathing answered the brusque greeting. "Bree!" the caller finally blustered. "Is she okay? Is she with you?"

Cam's insides relaxed. He held the phone out to his companion. "It's your brother. Sounds like he's about to hyperventilate."

Bree wrinkled her nose. "Like I told you, he'd heard already." She took the device from him and put it to her ear. "I'm fine, Dill."

"Where are you?"

Cam winced. Her brother must be shouting for the question to clearly reach him through the handset. Bree's scowl and pulling the instrument away from her face confirmed his deduction about her brother's volume.

"Dial it down, bro," she said, returning the phone to her ear. "Like I said, I'm entirely unhurt... Yes, Cam, too... No, it's better if you don't know where we are or what we're going to do next... Yup, I knew about the attack on ranger headquarters, but I'm not surprised it's on the news already."

Eavesdropping on the conversation between Bree and her brother was a bit like seeing the action of only one side of a volleyball court, but he could deduce the other end of the exchange. It was nice that Dillon had asked after him when his sister's situation had to be demanding every speck of concern in his heart.

"No, I can't come home... Yes, I know you'd do anything and everything to protect me, but it's not going to be enough. We have to face facts." The last part of the sentence emerged with a strangled sob. She took in a stuttering breath and her whole body stiffened as if coming to attention. "The Marshals Service is almost ready to take me into custody. I might never see you again, and that's just the way it has to be. I can't endanger—"

Dillon's outburst on the other end must have been more of a snarl than a shout since Cam couldn't make out the words, only the emphatic tone. Bree brought her mount to a halt and Cam did the same, scarcely daring to breathe as he awaited her response.

"I know you would willingly come with me, Dill." She hung her head, her shoulders suddenly slumping as if the weight of the world had finally crushed her. "I can't let you do that. I don't *want* you to do that. You've got a good life. Live it."

Cam bit down on the inside of his cheek and looked away, blinking against a salty sting in his eyes. Her situation was many times worse than his had been. She had someone who cared enough about her to give up his lifestyle and identity to be with her. No one had volunteered to enter exile with *him*. He envied Bree such a treasure of a relationship, and yet, the willingness of her loved one to sacrifice deepened the tragedy for them both. These siblings would miss each other terribly.

Cam mentally huffed. Doubtful that anyone was missing him from *his* former life. As bitter as that knowledge might taste on his tongue, at least the man he'd been was not the man he was now. He wouldn't go back to his shallow, self-centered old existence even if he could. A life-changing encounter with Jesus Christ had made him a new person even more thoroughly than a change of legal identity. And that was another part of his story he needed to share with Bree before the marshals took her away.

Cam's heart tore. Now, they'd never have the opportunity to explore what might have developed between them if given time and proximity. Their attraction was palpable and growing.

"Cam."

The voice barely impinged on his consciousness.

"Cameron Wolfe."

Bree's exasperated tone pierced Cam's introspection. He shuddered and met her bemused gaze. She'd put the satellite phone away, so he'd missed the end of her conversation with her brother, but he could infer the sorrow.

"I'm so sorry."

"Me, too." She gave a curt nod, set her face like stone and nudged her horse into motion.

Cam followed suit, any further words dying on his tongue. What else was there to say?

Within a half hour of steady, quiet riding, they came upon a small group of cows and calves ambling along in search of good grass and a drink of water. Like cowhands that had worked together for ages rather than a few days, Cam took one side of the grouping while Bree migrated to the other side, and they guided the small herd to a gate that let them into the furthest north pasture of Diamond-W property.

"Only about another hour, and we'll be there," he told Bree as she followed the cattle through the gate that he was holding open.

She nodded without a word, her face slack with weariness. The sun wouldn't go down for a while yet, but he had little doubt she was ready to collapse. The emotional toll of this day had been far greater than the physical. Nor had the blows finished coming. They expected any moment for the sat phone to ring with the Marshals Service on the other end with final arrangements to announce. Who knew? They might show up in a helicopter and whisk her away yet tonight.

Something like cold feathers slid across Cam's skin. His head knew the score, but his heart remained in denial. Wasn't there some other way? There hadn't been for him, but— Cam shook himself physically as he let himself through the gate and latched it. He needed to stop dreaming about what could never be and get his head in the here and now.

All too soon, the one-room cabin, standing squat and shabby like a forlorn sentinel on the bare prairie, came into view. Scenting water nearby, the herd quickened their hooves, though some moved in fits and starts, snatching mouthfuls of good green grass as they progressed toward the spring.

Pulling his horse up near the shack's front door that sagged on its hinges, Cam watched Bree for her reaction.

She snorted a ragged chuckle. "You told me the place wasn't much, and I see you may have exaggerated. There's 'not much,' and then there's 'hardly anything.' Are you sure the structure isn't going to collapse on our heads?"

Cam grinned at her. "The cabin is sturdier than it looks. I'm torn between thoughts of giving it a little tender loving care and bringing it to useful life again or leveling it. There's even a crude stone-walled root cellar beneath the structure and a cool room hollowed out of stone for preserving meat. Maybe our stay here will help make up my mind."

Bree swung down from her horse and Cam followed her example. In short order, they had the saddles and bridles off their mounts and stored in the lean-to that abutted the square structure. They gave their mounts and the pack-horse some quick brushes to get the worst of the sweat and dirt off for their comfort and so the animals wouldn't look like they'd recently been ridden. Then they turned the horses loose to mingle with the cows at the spring a short way behind the cabin.

"Shall we?" Cam motioned with his hand at the front door as he hefted a pannier of supplies.

"You first." Bree lifted the other pannier. "I'm not sure I'm that brave."

Cam chuckled and stepped up onto the short porch fronting the building. The place wasn't locked. Not much point in it when one of the windows was broken. He simply turned the knob and pushed the door open. An assortment of odors rushed him—dust and must and a bit of musk. Almost certainly, they'd have to chase out a small critter or two before they settled in.

To her credit, Bree didn't flinch or even mention the possibility—er, probability—of ro-dents. Despite her teasing about not being brave enough to step inside first, she was a ranch girl through and through. An hour later, they had their crude camp established. Matching sleeping bags had been rolled out against opposite walls of the cabin. A small propane camp stove for heating hot beverages or canned stew or beans was set up atop the wood-burning oven they had no plans to use. Canned and dry goods sat sorted on the counter and, finally, the sandwiches and cake Estrella had sent with them for the first meal had been laid out on the table. With matching groans, they settled on the rickety dining chairs to quiet their bellies' complaints.

Cam's muscles ached from the strange and strenuous day they had experienced. Her aches and pains were likely worse, considering she'd gone hand-to-hand with a *sicario*.

"How are you doing?" he asked her as they polished off the cake. "Physically, I mean. I know you're struggling emotionally. Who wouldn't be?"

She shrugged, keeping her eyes averted. "I'll probably be stiff and sore in the morning, but nothing too bad." Then her eyes snapped toward him.

Cam's face heated under the intensity of her stare.

"Don't you have a story to tell me?"

"Would you like to get some rest first? My tale can wait until morning if you're on overload."

"No more delay." The thrust of her chin and the steel of her gaze brooked no deflection.

Cam inhaled a deep breath and then let the oxygen trickle in miserly dribbles from his lungs. Time to come clean.

TEN

"Everett Davison."

At Cam's emphatic tone and his steady stare, Bree stiffened. The name Davison did ring a familiar bell in the back of her mind, but the details were fuzzy. Some sort of historical figure and something more current as well. She drew her brows together and sifted through her memories from lessons about the American Southwest.

"Start with Elliot…" Cam verbally prompted, and the picture snapped into focus in Bree's mind.

"Elliot Davison, the famous—some would say infamous—cattle baron from the late 1800s in New Mexico Territory. He gobbled up great swathes of land by any means necessary under his Leaning-D brand. Then, sitting on top of the world and poised to become the first governor of the newly formed state in 1912, he died suddenly of a heart attack."

Cam grinned at her, but a certain grimness

remained in his eyes. "You recall your South-western history lessons. Elliot's son, Ethan, took the dynasty to a new level with the discovery of oil on the Davison property. However, he never entered politics, though he meant to, but he also died before the dream could be realized."

"Right." Bree nodded. "By the third generation, the Davison name was pretty much synonymous with ranch royalty, and the fourth-generation patriarch, Emeric Davison, became a New Mexico state senator with his eyes on the US senate and maybe beyond. But didn't I hear a few years ago that the dynasty fell apart? Wasn't Emeric Davison found to be complicit in smuggling drugs and people from Mexico? There was a shootout on the property with the Ortega cartel, and people were killed, including Emeric."

A bright flicker of—what? pain?—lit Cam's eyes, but the emotion was extinguished so quickly Bree couldn't be certain she'd read the response correctly.

"Your recall is spot on." Cam nodded, his expression stoic. "The Leaning-D brand is now defunct, and the property either confiscated by the state or sold off by a scattered gaggle of shirt-tail heirs scrambling to distance themselves from a nasty scandal."

Bree frowned. "So, who is Everett Davison?"

"Me." Cam sat stiffly as if an iron rod had been attached to his spine.

Bree gaped at him.

"At least, I used to be." His lips pressed together into a thin line and his gaze fell away.

"Your real name is Everett Davison?" Bree blinked at him. "And you are a member of *that* Davison family?"

"Yes, to the latter. Emeric's only child and direct heir, in fact, but no, to the former. Everett Davison *used* to be my name. I am now legally Cameron Wolfe. According to a private bit of family lore, my several times great-grandmother's maiden name was Wolfe. Camille was a kind and Godly woman, by all accounts, and not a fan of her husband Elliot's tactics in chasing after riches. When I was forced into hiding, I wanted to connect back to an ancestral line with positive associations and yet have a name that was unlikely to be linked with my prior identity."

"Wow!" Bree lifted her camp mug to her lips and sucked in a deep draught of cool spring water to counteract a mouth suddenly gone dry. Then she clanked the metal cup onto the rough-hewn table. "You must have a long story to tell. So, give." She narrowed her eyes on Cameron—no, Everett—no, Cameron. At least, that was who he claimed to be now.

Cam's face reddened under her glare. He

heaved a great sigh and shook his head. "It *is* a long story and not a pretty one. I'm here now, living the simple, rural life that suits me, and I hope, with an integrity too many of my ruthless ancestors lacked."

Bree's heart panged at the anguish in his tone. He'd seen some ugliness, that was for sure, but how much of the mess he'd been exposed to, he had yet to disclose. "Were you there at the end for the gunfight?"

"I was." Raw anguish masked his face. No mistaking the pain this time. "I got this from a close-quarters knife fight in the melee." He brushed his fingertips across the scar on his face.

Silence fell, and Cam slurped a drink from his cup. Bree held her gaze on him, waiting quietly for him to gather himself and proceed.

Cam set his mug on the table and nudged it reflexively one way and then the other with the fingertips of opposite hands. "I was the inadvertent catalyst for the implosion of my family and the fallout that hurt some and helped others, but the chain of events started years before that senseless gun battle. How to begin…where to begin?"

His face went slack, as if he were meditating deeply, and then his jaw firmed and he met Bree's eyes. "Young Everett's mother divorced his father when he was six years old. She took her financial settlement and left him with his dad. He hardly ever saw her after that. You would think the situation would cause father and son to grow close, but that's not what happened." He let out a thin chuckle.

Bree opened her mouth to speak, but he lifted a forestalling hand, so she closed it again.

"Everett was a bit of a throwback child," he continued, "at least as far as his father was concerned. He took to ranch life like an eagle to the air. Not the ordering-things-done-from-the-office, cattle-baron lifestyle, emulating the dad he never clicked with, but the hands-on, nitty-gritty work of wrangling cattle and horses, imitating the ranch foreman he followed around like a gangly puppy.

"Daddy Emeric didn't approve, but he was too wrapped up in his own busy schedule to interfere much when the boy was little. He had visions of his son realizing the family dream of going big into politics, and he maneuvered like a Formula One racing driver to make the kind of social connections that would set his son up for success. Emeric did so well at it that he ended up a state senator himself. The only rain on his parade was young Everett refusing to engage in politics in his footsteps. The contentiousness got so heated that as soon as Everett was old enough, he left his beloved ranch."

"Ouch!" Bree leaned forward and touched Cam's knee. "That must have hurt."

"Like an infected wisdom tooth." He nodded. "But then, Everett found his second great career love, law enforcement. He ended up a DEA agent."

"Wait a second." Bree sat back in her chair. "I thought you told me you 'cooperated' with the DEA in taking down a human-smuggling ring, not that you were an agent yourself."

He grimaced with a shake of the head. "At the time of the events at the Leaning-D, I was no longer a DEA agent—but we're getting ahead of the story."

"So, you were a civilian when the bullets were flying at the ranch? Just like now with all we've been dealing with?" Bree's gut went hollow. "Living through this situation with me now has got to be like a nightmare déjà vu."

"You have no idea how accurate your assessment is. There's more. A lot more." The words emerged in a taut, inflectionless string. All color drained from Cam's face and his hands resting on the tabletop formed white-knuckled fists.

"I'm listening. Go on." She resisted the urge to reach out to him again.

A comforting touch wasn't welcome at this moment. She'd been there herself when the pain was too raw and the slightest well-meaning sympathy would trigger protective walls snapping into place to contain the hurt. If Cam was going to get through this tale, she needed to let him tell the story at his pace.

For him, speaking it out loud could also be a form of processing trauma. Bree knew that well enough from the aftermath of her failed relationship with her ex-husband. At least she had enjoyed a childhood of close family life with loving parents. Apparently, Cam was unacquainted with that priceless benefit. How he'd turned into the fine man she'd come to know and appreciate, Bree could scarcely comprehend.

"Unbeknownst to our stalwart hero—" Cam let out a self-mocking chuckle "—Daddy had a secret weapon in his arsenal by the name of Tessa Harding. And, boy, was she the nuclear option. She blew poor Everett's life compass off the map. For her, he'd give up what she called 'the risky law enforcement life.' He'd even return to the ranch where Senator Papa waited with his agenda. Everything was going to plan for Tessa and Emeric, and then the ranch got ahold of Everett once more.

"He realized he'd come home, and he wasn't going to leave again for any sort of campaign trail or the halls of government. In fact, the socialite life that was oxygen for Tessa polluted Everett's nostrils like toxic fumes. Tessa and

Papa pitched all kinds of fits, so Everett started spending days at a time out on the range, wrestling with his fascinated devotion to Tessa, his loathing for the political machinations that invigorated his father, and his need to make some sort of peace with all of it that didn't involve him selling his soul. That's when he restarted his childhood habit of reading his generations-removed-grandmother's Bible by campfire light."

Something long dormant in Bree's heart stirred and she shifted uncomfortably in her seat. "Camille Wolfe's Bible?"

"Yep."

"Did the reading help?"

"Beyond my wildest dreams. Reading through the Gospels and my dear ancestor's notes in the margins overhauled my thinking and set me free from my problems without changing my circumstances one iota."

Bree's facial muscles tensed. "What do you mean by that?"

"Jesus made Himself real to me in those pages and confronted me with my selfishness."

"Selfishness?" Bree snorted. "Sounds like you were in the fight for your life as you needed it to be."

"Exactly. *My* life as *I* wanted it to be. Absolutely self-centered, fighting tooth and nail for *my* way. But this newfound awareness of my own failures didn't mean I needed to surrender to other people's selfish agendas. No, I needed to listen to the One who has always had my best interests at heart. I had never given two minutes thought to what God might want from me and for me. To say I was humbled and stunned was putting it mildly."

Suddenly consumed with a need to know what had come from this personal epiphany, Bree leaned toward Cam. "What did you do?"

He laughed, a free and light sound that contrasted starkly with his dark mood moments before. "I stayed in camp with no other humans around for three more terrible, wonderful days."

"Terrible?"

"Yes, the most horrifically excellent days of my life. God shone a spotlight on my life, confronting me with all the specific instances where I trampled others or disregarded them to advance myself. I had a stellar record with the DEA, not just because I was a good agent—which I was— but because I didn't care who I hurt or slighted to make a success of my career. I *had* to show Daddy I would make something of myself without his influence or his money. Under Divine scrutiny, I was horrified by the callous person I'd become. By the time I was done humbling myself and repenting in that remote campsite on the backside of nowhere, I felt clean and whole for the first time in my life."

Bree's insides roiled. What should she make of this raw testimony? Surely, all this humbling and repenting didn't apply to *her* life, did it? Just because she'd stopped being a church-goer after the divorce— She ruthlessly shut down that avenue of introspection. Her wounds were her own to lick. God understood that, didn't He?

Cam's eyes glowed and he let out another laugh. "Just the memory of that special time basking in the Lord's presence reminds me again to stop focusing on myself or negative situations."

"Sounds terrific." Bree snorted. "I wish that were an option for me."

Cam's unguarded yet unflinching stare riveted Bree to her seat. "Isn't it?"

Her insides curled away from the soul-baring look as if Someone else were gazing into her depths through his eyes. What did He see?

She knew. Yes, in the secret place of her heart, she knew He'd found the fears and insecurities that kept her presenting a tough face to the world and guarding every scrap of independence like her own personal Fort Knox. What would happen between herself and God, between herself and this man, if she let her guard down? Did she have the courage to find out?

* * *

From the expression on her face, something he'd said had disturbed Bree deeply. Not his intention in his soul-baring. He'd only been seeking to communicate clearly. But her eyes darting here and there, settling on nothing, and the flatness of her expression betrayed discomfort and probably a significant inner battle. What that meant related to what he'd told her, Cam had no way of knowing. Had she suddenly started to mistrust him because of the faults he'd confessed?

"It's okay." He lifted a hand in a placating gesture. "I'm not expecting anything from you, and I'm not about to skip out. I'm here for the duration."

Bree's leaf-green eyes landed on him. "I know you're not leaving, but I still don't understand why not."

"Maybe it would help if I finished my story. I haven't spoken of this to anyone since the debrief with law enforcement after the shootout."

"How long ago was that?"

"Two years of hiding and wandering. It's taken me this long to work through all the legalities in a way that didn't leave a public record for the Ortega cartel find and to locate a new place to call home."

Bree frowned down into her empty mug. "I appreciate you being willing to tell me about a horribly painful incident, and I want to hear it." She rose from her rickety seat, her gaze doing that darting thing again. "But I need some time to process what you've told me so far. Besides, I'm bushed. Can it wait until tomorrow morning?"

In the growing dimness of the unlit room at dusk, Cam studied her weary posture and took note of the dark circles under her eyes. "Sure. Get some rest. We can go at this fresh tomorrow. Who knows? Maybe inspiration will strike and we'll come up with some ingenious way of thwarting the Ortega cartel permanently without uprooting you from your life."

Bree let out a sound like a cross between a snicker and a snort. "I won't be holding my breath while I'm dreaming of rainbows and lollipops."

Cam laughed. "Fair enough. I'm all for being realistic, but I'm not giving up either."

He busied himself cleaning their food mess and putting away the few eating utensils they'd used while Bree sat down on her sleeping bag and removed her boots. Then she curled up on top of the sleeping bag with her back toward Cam. The cabin was too warm and stuffy to allow for slumber inside covers.

His eyes swept the small, musty room. The sun was down, but the moon was bright, and objects indoors had become hazy shadows. To avoid exposing the cabin's occupancy, they could not light a lamp. Turning in for the night made sense. But first he moved carefully to the gaping hole left by the broken window and peered out into the night.

Slowly moving lumps of darkness betrayed livestock ambling across the grass. In the near distance, a cow mooed, probably summoning a wayward calf. Insects hummed, a few flitting by him into their meager shelter, along with a breeze barely cooler than the still-warm, sage-laden air on the cusp between summer and fall on the Llano Estacado.

Not long now, and the temperature would fall significantly. Winter wasn't a time to be caught roughing it on the Llano prairie. A resolution for Bree's situation needed to be found and acted upon swiftly. If only it didn't appear her single viable option was disappearing into witness protection. He would miss her more than made any sense to him, considering the short time they'd been acquainted.

Was there anything he could do to change what seemed the inevitable course of events? After all, he was acquainted with Alonzo Espinoza. Some might even think the drug lord owed him a favor. Cam let out a muted snort. Doubtful Espinoza did the math that way after all that had happened. Besides, reaching out to the head of the Espinoza cartel risked exposing himself to the Ortega faction. It was widely known that the rival cartels had spies embedded in each other's organizations. But did the risk outweigh the potential benefit if Alonzo was inclined to listen to Cam's—er, Everett's plea for clemency toward Bree? He would have to reach out under his old identity. A shudder ran through Cam's body.

With a sigh, he turned away from the window. He should get some shuteye, too. If a person or a machine came within the vicinity of the line shack, the animals would be disturbed and their sounds of alarm would wake him up.

Cam removed his boots and then lay down atop his bag, which did little to soften the hard floor. Sleeping outside on the ground might have been marginally more comfortable. Maybe they could do that tomorrow night, weather permitting.

Sleep proved elusive. Like chasing happiness, it darted away just beyond his reach the more he strained for it. Finally, he sat up and scrubbed his eyes with the heels of his hands.

"Cam?" Bree's soft voice reached him across the dark space that separated them.

"Yup."

"You can't sleep either?"

He chuckled. "Nope."

A rustling came from the opposite side of the shack and her shadowy form sat up and turned toward him, her face half lit by the moonlight seeping in through the window opening. "I think I need to hear the rest of your story. What happened to Everett Davison on the Leaning-D in New Mexico that has Cameron Wolfe ranching in Texas on the Diamond-W?"

He swallowed against a dry throat. Might as well throw the punch line out there. "Everett Davison saved Alonzo Espinoza's daughter's life."

"What?" The question came out a strangled screech. "No way! Why did you save that piece of information until now? How? You have some explaining to do."

Her incredulous outrage brought a grin to Cam's face that quickly fell away as he considered the rest of the tale he was about to share. He rested his back against the wall of the shack and let his mind roam into the past. How could he encapsulate a wild jumble of actions and reactions into a few intelligible sentences?

"The day I broke camp from my life-changing retreat on the range and began my return to ranch headquarters," he began in low, slow tones, "I ran smack into a hidden compound of human traffickers in a remote area of the Leaning-D. They had a shack not much nicer than this one located in a snug little canyon. A trio of armed thugs were in the process of herding a group of teenagers and children out of the building and into a small haulage truck fitted for off-road travel. I was on a ridge overlooking the activity, and they didn't spot me. Naturally, I wasn't about to let them get away with their human contraband."

"Of course not, but what could you do? You were all alone."

Cam shrugged, though she probably couldn't see the gesture. "There were only three bad guys, but the situation was tricky because I didn't want to give them an opportunity to harm the kids, which they might do if they felt cornered. Let's condense the story and say I got out ahead of them and arranged for some sharp objects to give their truck a flat tire. While a pair of them were replacing the tire, I crept in and knocked the one guarding the children unconscious. Then it was easy to get the drop on the other two because they'd had to lay aside their weapons to change the flat."

"Just another day at the office? Not hardly!" Bree laughed. "Don't tell me. One of the children was Alonzo Espinoza's daughter. *You're* the guy who thwarted Raul Ortega's plot to revenge himself on his arch rival by taking his enemy's youngest child. Law enforcement kept your name out of the news."

"Got it in one guess."

Something like a growl came from Bree's throat. "I hate it when innocents get caught up in evil grown-ups' vicious games."

"Me, too. If I didn't *know* that somehow no suffering goes to waste and that Divine justice will ultimately and eternally be served, I would be in despair over humanity and this messed-up world. Not that I have any easy answers about bad things happening to innocents, but at least I can now say I trust the One who does. That wasn't always the case."

"Hmm." A floorboard creaked as Bree shifted to a new position. "I don't think I'm where you're at yet on the subject, but let's move on. What happened next?"

"Fair enough." Cam lifted a silent prayer for Bree to make her peace with God. At least, he was wise enough to know praying was the best thing he could do. How the struggle between bitterness and faith came out was an intensely personal thing. "Oddly, after the authorities came and hauled the creeps away and took custody of the trafficked children, my father joined me in lobbying for my name to be kept out of the news releases. I thought he'd leap on the incident as an opportunity to thrust me forward into the limelight or at least to toot his own political agenda as a law enforcement advocate. The reaction to avoid publicity was highly suspicious to anyone who knew Emeric Davison. That's when I first began to dread that my father knew something about the trafficking that was happening on his property. To say I was torn up about the idea would be an understatement."

A soft, whining sigh came from Bree's side of the cabin, her sympathy unspoken but clear. "Completely understandable."

"I wish I could say that was the end of the story and my suspicions subsided." A sour taste formed on his tongue. "But things escalated and got more complicated from there. The one bright ray in the murky mess was that all the children were returned to their families, including Espinoza's daughter. Cartel chief or not, the US wasn't about to withhold his daughter from him. What a political nightmare that would be. The other side of the coin is that my name got back to Espinoza as his daughter's savior and to Raul Ortega as the one who thwarted his act of vengeance on his arch rival."

"Yikes!" Bree let out a low whistle. "All of a sudden, you got plopped into the middle of a blood feud between ruthless men."

"Brianna Maguire, you are perspicacious as always." Cam laced his tone with irony. "The end of the nightmare for those kids was just the beginning for me. I—"

"Shh!"

Bree's sudden shush froze the words in Cam's throat.

"Do you hear that?" Her words were an urgent whisper.

Cam held his breath and strained his ears. Outside, the cattle's lowing grew more frequent, and hooves thudded on the hard ground. Not stampeding, but uneasily milling. Then above the animal sounds, a faint, unnatural buzz sent chills cascading through his body and stood his hair on end.

A drone had found them. Or maybe not found them...yet. But the eyes in the sky were searching, and if the mechanical creature was roaming in the dark, the equipment must include night vision and possibly infrared capabilities. Their heat signatures inside the cabin would glow brightly, a place where the livestock would not be.

Cam rose and snatched up his rifle, boots and saddlebags. "Down into the stone cool room beneath the cabin. Now!"

Wordlessly, Bree grabbed the same items and followed him to the trap door against the far wall. Something like frozen barbed wire twisted Cam's insides. They had seconds to disappear into the manmade stone cavern—if that long. Their response to the incursion might already be too late.

ELEVEN

As Cam flung the cellar door wide open, Bree's pulse thundered so loudly in her ears that the smack of the door against the floorboards barely registered with her. A black hole gaped inches beyond her sock-clad feet. Ice congealed in her middle.

How could she make herself jump down in there? How deep was the pit? Did any creepy crawlies, or worse, a venomous snake, await her?

A snap near at hand drew her attention and a muted, blue glow flowed around them, not likely visible outside the cabin. Cam had activated a glow stick, no doubt from his pack. He tossed the stick below, and an expanse, void of any threatening creatures, took shape. The dirt floor of the cellar lay about six feet beneath the shack, and there was a rickety-looking ladder, which they didn't have time to test or use.

Inhaling a deep breath, Bree jumped into the hole then swiftly moved out of Cam's way as he did the same while pulling the trap door shut. Dust puffed up around them, and a musty, damp odor pervaded the space. Bree bottled a sneeze.

Cam scooped up the glow stick and jabbed it in the direction of the cellar's far wall. The area continued longer than where the cabin's outer wall must extend, and the rough-hewn, mortared rock walls gave way to the solid, human-chiseled stone of what might have been a tiny natural cavern before people had fashioned it for use as a cool room. The nearby spring may have originally carved the hollow in the rock, though the water no longer flowed there.

Crouching, Bree scuttled toward the cover of the stone alcove where no heat signature could betray them to those who hunted their lives. Cam did the same, his height forcing him to bend nearly double to avoid hitting his head on the ceiling. Breathing raggedly and huddled together, they pressed themselves against the farthest wall of the small cavern.

Their escape into the earth had consumed mere seconds. But had they been fast enough to avoid detection? They would have to wait to find out. But for how long did they dare crouch here, cornered with no way out, if they had been detected and armed enemies even now converged on their location?

Cam stirred and began tugging his boots onto his stockinged feet.

"Good idea," Bree murmured and copied him.

Now they were ready to move at a moment's notice, but they had nowhere to go. A bitter taste invaded Bree's mouth. Is this what their lives had come to? Crouching in a hole, waiting to be discovered and snuffed out?

No, she didn't dare think such hopeless thoughts.

But what hope did she truly have left? If they escaped this cabin with their lives, she had days or maybe only hours before she would be torn from everything and everyone she had ever known in order to be relocated where no one and nothing was familiar. Cam's assistance to her must surely be common knowledge now. Did that mean he would need to uproot himself and run again, also?

Bree's heart did a little hop. Could they go away together? No, wait, that was silly. They barely knew each other. Why would he want to tie himself to her for the foreseeable future? How ironic that doing what was right in bringing evildoers to justice during that shootout with the rustlers would end up wrecking her life and damaging her brother, her work colleagues, and her new neighbor in a cascade of consequences.

There must be a solution. What am I not seeing?

Her only answer came in outer silence, marked by the solemn thudding of her heart.

Next to her, Cam stirred and drew himself up into a cross-legged, seated posture with his back resting against the stone wall. "We may be wise to spend the rest of the night here."

Bree let out a groan. "I hate this fleeing-and-hiding routine. I so badly want to bring the fight to the crooks, but going on the offensive against a monster criminal machine like a cartel is sure suicide."

"Isn't going on the offensive what law enforcement is all about?"

"Sure, but the legal apparatus is a behemoth in itself, designed to take on the worst of the worst." She assumed a similar posture to his and hugged herself against the chill of this microcavern that felt more and more like a tomb. "When an individual is singled out for attention from the criminal element, the whole balance of the struggle is taken out of the equation. You, of all people, know this. What's your point?"

"My point is since we're cooling our heels down here—literally—I should probably finish my story. I have the glimmerings of an idea, but I want to see if you discern it also."

"An idea? Really?" Bree squinted at her companion. The glow from the stick was fading, leaving more shadow than light in their alcove.

"It's extremely dangerous, and you're going

to hate it—though probably marginally less than your current alternative of witness protection."

"Stop with the teasing already and tell me."

"The end of the story first."

"No rush. I've got all night."

At her dry tone, Cam chuckled, and Bree managed a slight smile, her heart lightening marginally. This man was truly extraordinary. Everything in her wanted to get to know him better. The usual flashing red light of stop-and-go wariness when she considered a potential new relationship had flipped to solid yellow with flickers of green sometime during the past weeks' idyll spent living and working alongside him on his ranch.

During one of their long conversations, she'd even opened up enough to share the bare facts with him surrounding her prior marriage and its ending. His compassionate response, minus any hint of pity, had left her with the sense he had reason to understand her pain. She'd like to know more details about his past relationships that would have given rise to that impression, but she hadn't pried. As they continued to get to know one another, she trusted the subject would be explored in due course—provided they were given enough time.

Going into WITSEC would end the possibilities instantly. If Cam's nascent idea had any merit at all, she would have to leap into the project with both feet.

Maybe. Her old habit of caution nudged her.

"Where did I leave off?" Cam asked.

"Your name got outed to both the Espinoza and Ortega cartels. I can guess the consequences. Espinoza wanted to reward you and Ortega wanted to kill you."

"Right on both counts. Alonzo's version of rewarding me was summoning me to a face-to-face meeting with him."

"And you went?"

"One tends to comply when you're grabbed off the street and thrown into the back of an SUV at gunpoint."

"Friendly!"

"Exactly what cartels are famous for."

They snickered almost in unison.

"The guy really did think he was being magnanimous when he offered to bring me in on his move to take over the Ortega smuggling route that went straight across Leaning-D range, especially when he pledged not to traffic humans, only drugs."

"Why would Espinoza think you'd be interested in replacing one cartel with another in exploiting your property?"

Silence fell for a heartbeat as Cam visibly cringed in the fading illumination of the glow stick. "Apparently, my adversarial relationship with my father was common knowledge. Alonzo thought I would enjoy betraying him while enveloping myself and my ranch under Espinoza protection."

Bree gasped as the implications cascaded over her. "In effect, you would become a puppet of the Espinoza cartel, dependent upon it as a shield. Plus, the offer revealed that—"

"My father was actively cooperating with the Ortega cartel." The words snarled from Cam's mouth. "Up until that moment, standing before Alonzo Espinoza, I had only suspected the worst. Clung to a shred of hope that it wasn't so. Now I knew, and I could no longer pretend my family name possessed a shred of honor."

"Oh, Cam, how devastating." She released a deep groan. "Intending to do you a favor, Espinoza wounded you deeper than a bullet from an Ortega gun."

"Thank you." Cam hung his head. "It means a lot to me that you understand."

"Of course."

Cam seemed to shake himself, and he lifted his chin and met her gaze. "Naturally, I turned down the so-generous offer. I half expected a shallow grave to follow my defiance, but Alonzo declared he was releasing me with my life for saving his daughter, but to expect no further favors."

"Right! You saved his daughter from untold horrors, but the best he could offer in response was to *not* kill you when you turned down a so-called business opportunity. How messed up is that?"

"Twisted thoughts are a symptom of a dark heart."

"Deep. Almost sounds like a Scripture verse, but I don't recall the quote."

"It's not directly from the Bible, though the principle is there. The incident with Alonzo Espinoza did remind me of the verse from Proverbs that says, 'The tender mercies of the wicked are cruel.' The context is the care of animals, but to cartel leaders, people are cattle to be exploited."

"I can't disagree there. Where's this idea of yours? I thought, for a minute, you were going to offer to contact Alonzo Espinoza and trade my safety for the favor he owes you for saving his daughter. But now it sounds like that obligation is off the table, at least in Espinoza's reckoning. Not that I'd want you to risk yourself making a deal with the sort of human snake that would turn around and bite you as soon as false promises escaped his mouth." As the last of the light from the glow stick winked out, Bree's gaze linked with Cam's. Was that tenderness in his expression? Her heart fluttered. "What?"

"You are a remarkable woman. A genuine protector and person of integrity. I'm blessed to have met you."

Thankfully, the inky atmosphere hid the hot flush that washed Bree's face. Involuntarily, she leaned closer to him. He must be doing the same because his warm breath touched her lips. Anticipation of the earth-moving kiss tingled through her. And then—

The world exploded in heat, light and thunder. Pain splintered her psyche and the relief of nothingness swallowed her whole.

The explosion's brilliance seared Cam's eyeballs and he squeezed his lids closed even as he threw himself at Bree. Too late to spare her much except to absorb the brunt of the falling rubble. Dislodged stones pelted him and bits of hot rubble stung his back. A muted roar, snap and crackle let him know that fire was actively consuming the main portion of the cabin. At least, in the stone alcove, they were sheltered from the worst of the flames, though the heat washed in waves across him. Smoke bit his lungs and he coughed.

Pulling the bandana around his neck up across his mouth and nose, he pulled away from Bree onto his elbows. She lay limp on the ground. Cam's heart stuttered. He opened his watering eyes and scanned her pale face in the flickering gloom.

"Bree!"

He quickly touched her throat and found a pulse. Then he put a finger close to her nose and her exhales puffed around it. *Thank You, God.* She was alive, at least, but how injured he had yet to determine.

Somehow fresh air mingled with the smoke, alternately providing good breaths and tainted breaths, depending on the fluctuations of the breeze that swirled around them. Still coughing, Cam sat up and looked around. The cabin had collapsed entirely into the cellar, and the God-created night sky glimpsed between burning wreckage replaced the shattered, human-made roof.

A deep groan, followed by a wracking cough, came from the woman beside him. She stirred and attempted to sit up.

Cam pressed her down with a hand on her shoulder. "Take it easy until we see where you're hurt."

Bree's eyelids fluttered. "Where I'm hurt? Try everywhere. And nowhere, too. I think it was just the concussion of…whatever that was."

"You have a concussion?"

"That's not what I meant." She rubbed her forehead, smearing dirt and soot. "It was the pressure, like being crushed by a wall of super-heated air."

"That's what explosions are like." Cam slumped beside her. His own wounds smarted, but so far he didn't think anything major had been injured. He'd know more when the adrenaline wore off and they tried to move. "I think we can safely deduce our presence in the cabin was detected, but unless someone was standing out there with an RPG to shoot at us, I'm fairly sure we were hit remotely by an actual kamikaze drone."

"Not like the regular drone that hit Dillon's pickup truck."

"Correct."

Bree sat up with a high whine and gritted teeth. "Then our attackers think they got us."

"I'm sure they're hoping so, but I'm equally sure they'll send someone to check and confirm. Probably in the morning."

"Then we need to get out of here as quickly as possible."

Cam frowned at the dying fires dotting the main cellar area. "As soon as it's safe to move out of this microcavern and climb the stone wall."

"Our horses." Her eyes went wide. "They will have run away from the explosion."

"No doubt, but I hope they didn't go far. I

think the spring of water will draw them back in this direction, at least by morning. How are you at riding bareback? I assume our saddles are toast."

"We'll manage." Bree suddenly hiccupped on a catch of breath. "Oh, Cam!" She threw her arms around him and sobbed. "Again…we made it through an attack…but we can't…survive much longer."

"We'll either have to get you into witness protection, or we'll need to stage a showdown."

"Stage a what?" She pulled away from him, moonlit tears glistening on a pair of scowling cheeks.

"It's either full retreat with the hope that you're never found wherever the Marshals Service places you, or we take control of the situation and draw the enemy to us where he—or rather, *they*—can be neutralized."

She scrunched her eyebrows together and glared at him. "You want to lure Alonzo Esperanza *here*?"

"Not here, necessarily, but to the United States at a place of our choosing. And not just Alonzo, but Raul Ortega as well. We won't get one without the other."

"How do you propose to pull off that feat?"

"You are the bait for Alonzo, and I am the bait for Raul, and they are the irresistible lure for each other. If they each think they are going to be able to get their targets of revenge and take out their rival forever in one fell swoop, neither one will be able to resist showing up in person on this side of the US/Mexico border. Then, if we're prepared and waiting for them, they can be arrested and locked up where they belong."

She gaped at him like a beached fish and then suddenly snapped her jaw closed and scowled. "I hate the idea."

"I knew you would."

"It's going to be so dangerous."

"Yup."

"Let's do it."

Cam grinned. He couldn't help himself. "I knew you were going to say that, too."

Bree swatted him on the arm and he winced at a stab of pain.

"You *are* hurt." She moved closer to him, scanning him up and down.

"Scorched by sparks here and there and bruised from flying debris. But since I don't seem to be bleeding out, we need to get as far away from here as we can before more enemies arrive. We can assess injuries and perform first aid later."

"Gotcha." She scooted toward the opening of the stone hollow with her rifle in one hand and her saddlebags in the other.

Cam opened his mouth to call her back and insist on venturing into the still-smoldering wreckage first. Then he shut his jaw. Bree was a trained Texas Ranger. She knew how to handle herself in risky situations.

He scuttled out in her wake, acrid smoke biting the back of his throat, but not in health-threatening amounts. Gradually, they weaved around shattered pieces of furniture and shredded wall and floorboards. A shard of metal gleamed up at him from the devastation. Possibly a piece of the drone that had wrought this havoc.

They came to a cellar wall and Cam assessed the stones and masonry for hand-and footholds. They didn't need to climb up far. The cabin had been thoroughly leveled by the blast, so the top of his head came nearly even with the ground above.

Bree turned to him. "Just make a stirrup with your hands. I can step into it, and you can hoist me up. Then I'll turn and grab the supplies from you."

"Sounds like a plan."

Cam did as she asked, and soon she crawled onto terra firma with a groan that hinted she had a few bumps and bruises herself. Lying on her stomach, she reached down, and he handed her his rifle and bags. Using the holds he'd spotted, he hauled himself out of the hole that used to be a cellar. A moment later, he flopped down beside Bree. The cool grass soothed his slightly fried back.

She got to her feet and did a slow 360-degree turn. "I don't see hide nor hair of livestock. Which way would you guess the horses went?"

"Whichever direction got them away the fastest from the danger." Gritting his teeth against a pained hiss, Cam stood beside her. "But I doubt if they ran too far from water. If we want to catch them, I think we'll have to wait near the spring and hope they show up before the cartel scouting party arrives to confirm their kill."

Bree huffed. "I don't think we have a lot of choice. We need mounts to travel fast. Hoofing it cross-country in cowboy boots won't get us far enough away from here to avoid detection by the bad guys come morning. In fact, on foot and without cover on this prairie landscape, we'd be completely vulnerable."

"To the spring it is."

Cam led the way to the patch of wet ground that marked the tiny spring bubbling to the surface, tracing a short path across the terrain and then, just as quickly, diving underground again. Maybe he should dig a well here and tap into the aquifer that was clearly down there. He shook himself as he located a dense huddle of shrubbery where they could shelter and await the horses' return. Now was not the time for planning and dreams. Then again, why not think positively?

If their desperate ploy went awry, as it so easily might, this could be one of the last times he entertained practical dreams for his ranch. Failure to stop both Alonzo Espinoza and Raul Ortega meant no more future for Bree or for him. And certainly not for them together. For a reason he didn't care to examine at the moment, that thought hurt most of all.

TWELVE

Something cool and bristly brushed Bree's cheek and she swiped at it without opening her eyes. Whatever had disturbed her slumber went away and she drifted toward oblivion once more. Then the bristles feathered her skin again, accompanied by a loud, snuffling warm breath washing across her face. She jerked awake and sat up. Her sudden movement prompted a startled whicker and the thud of trotting hooves retreating. She turned her head to find a familiar equine rump moving away from her. What? Where was she?

"Teton!" Her involuntary cry drew Bree fully into the waking world.

The sky had begun to pale, revealing a sepia landscape dotted with grass clumps waving in a steady breeze. Heaviness tinged the air as if the environment were waiting for something momentous. A storm may be brewing, though as yet the clouds were scarce overhead.

Bree shook herself physically. How could she have fallen asleep after the events of last night? Curled up on the lumpy ground in the sparse cover of a juniper bush, no less? She shook herself. Why she'd fallen asleep didn't matter, though exhaustion and trauma probably explained it. What mattered was that the horses had returned, exactly as dawn was breaking, and they needed to vacate the area.

Battling the aches and pains of stiff muscles and bruised bones, Bree struggled to her feet, keeping a firm grip on the rifle she'd slept with clutched to her chest. Where was Cam? Her gaze scanned the area. Teton hadn't gone far—just to the edge of the spring, where he had stuck his nose in the water. Cattle also had gathered around, but no Cam and no Rojo, or the pack mare either.

Her throat tightened and her heart rate sped up. He wouldn't leave her. Had something happened? No, surely she wouldn't have slept through anything dramatic going on nearby. But maybe he'd left to look for the horses and run into the bad guys. No, that dire scenario didn't work either. At least, not very well. She'd heard no gunshots. However, if Cam had been threatened at gunpoint and captured, no one would necessarily have fired. Bree's head spun and she matched the movement with her body, searching in every direction as far as her eye could see in the growing light.

"Bree!"

Cam's distant call fell sweetly on her ears. Bree turned east and flung up a hand to shade her eyes from the sun's first piercing rays. She smiled. The man certainly did make a striking figure on horseback, even riding bareback without a saddle or bridle. He'd found Rojo, and the stallion was evidently well enough trained to allow him to mount and would accept guidance from knee pressure. The pack mare ambled along in the wake of the magnificent pair.

Bree waved and then scooped up her saddlebags and headed for the spring. At her approach, Teton lifted a dripping muzzle from the water and turned his head toward her, ears pricked in her direction. As she neared, he stepped out and met her.

"Hey, boy, did you have a scare last night?" She rubbed his muzzle then moved along his side, rubbing his shiny coat with her palm. The smoothness of his skin and the familiar horsey scent calmed her riled nerves. "You look like you're all right. No injuries from flying debris or anything."

Continuing to croon kind words, she stopped near his withers and hopped upward so she practically lay sideways over his back. Teton turned his head, ears waggling back and forth. Bree grinned at him and swung her leg over the top so that she ended up sitting in the spot where a saddle would have been. The bags sat awkwardly across her legs, but it was the only place for them where they wouldn't slip off, and the rifle rested in the crook of an elbow.

Winding the fingers of one hand through Teton's thick mane, she clucked at him and nudged him with a knee in the direction she wanted him to go. The gelding snorted, possibly a mild grumble at the odd arrangement, and headed for the approaching party of Cam, Rojo and pack mare. As soon as she and Teton converged with them, Bree brought the gelding to a halt, and Cam did the same with his stallion.

Her gaze narrowed on Cam. Now that she was close to him, his bedraggled condition became apparent. Dark ash smeared spots and stripes across his face. His jeans showed dirt and tears. And scorched holes on the arms and shoulders of his shirt exposed the red marks of first-degree burns.

Bree clucked her tongue. "You need treatment."

His teeth gleamed extra-white in his filthy face as he offered a grin. "Not to mention a bath, but first aid for minor injuries and other such luxuries are far down on my priority list. Let's grab a drink at the spring, fill up our canteens, and get far away from here." He tapped Rojo's ribs with his heels and moved toward the spring.

Bree followed without another word. Soon, humans and animals were hydrated and heading onto the prairie.

"This direction seems random." Bree shot her companion a sharp glance. "Where are we going?"

"For the moment, it *is* random. We need to get out of sight of the cabin. Where do you suggest for an ultimate destination?"

"Home. I just want to go home." She heaved in a deep breath and let it out slowly. "Do I sound pitiful?"

Cam shook his head. "You sound correct." His tender gaze soothed her raw nerves. "We'll have to sneak onto your ranch to avoid potentially hostile watching eyes, though, hopefully, they may already think we're dead and be gone. We need to talk to Dillon privately in person to recruit him into our plot to trap the cartel bosses."

"About that." Bree bit her lower lip. In the morning light, the idea appeared ludicrous, suicidal even.

"We'll talk further later. Let's move!" Cam kicked Rojo into a ground-eating lope.

Bree had no choice but to follow suit, though her gut churned in sync with writhing thoughts.

Or maybe her problem was hunger. They had jerky in their packs but no time to eat it until they were out of range of an aerial spotter heading for the destroyed cabin. Then again, the cartel might be in no hurry and opt for a low-key overland approach.

Hopefully, the latter. She'd had her fill of aerial threats. Besides, she and Cam would have more time to get away if the enemy were approaching overland. A growl formed in Bree's throat. She'd had her fill of running from danger, too. Maybe taking their lives in their hands and running toward the threat really was the only sensible option in this appalling scenario.

Gradually, the familiar thud of hooves against the ground and the rhythmic bunch and stretch of Teton's muscles beneath her lulled her tension. If the situation wasn't so dire, she could enjoy this ride. Her gelding loped, ears perked, and neck stretched out, his nose parallel to the stallion's haunches. Both animals seemed to feel the urgency, yet they were finding pleasure in the exercise, at least between gusts of wind that seemed to be growing more frequent and pelted them with dust. Teton snorted against the unpleasantness, and Bree fitted her bandana over her nose and mouth.

Then Cam's torso swiveled toward her and he pointed to their right. Bree turned her head, and her breath caught in her throat. In the distance, a streaky wall of blackness had formed, led by a hedge of wind-churned dust. Judging from a faint but growing rumble, the dense veil of water appeared to be rushing straight for them. The storm hinted at by the heavy air at dawn was here—a last hurrah of rain before long dry months arrived. Heavy rainstorms on the Llano were no joke. The force of the periodic deluges had dug the ravines, wadis and canyons that scarred the prairie and sometimes sent the rivers into devastating flood stage.

Instinctively, Bree nudged Teton away from the approaching storm. Even as she did so, a crack of thunder rolled across the plain with an accompanying flash of lightning. They couldn't hope to outrun the weather, but they needed time to locate some sort of shelter, however meager.

Rojo inserted himself in Teton's path. The gelding protested with a jerk of the head and a whinny, but he slowed to a walk. Bree clung precariously to her position atop a horse with no saddle.

"What was that for?" She scowled at Rojo's rider.

Cam's dark gaze flew skyward but not in the direction of the wild weather. Bree looked up. Ice stabbed her chest. A speck in the distance barely stood out from the gathering gloom, but she had no trouble recognizing a helicopter heading their way. The beat of its rotors had been masked by the rumble from the maw of the storm.

Bree fixed a grim gaze on her companion. "Our shelter is the storm itself. It's the only alternative. The chopper will have great difficulty flying in that weather, and whoever is inside the bird certainly won't be able to spot us."

Cam's lips quirked into a wry half smile. "So, we choose the lesser of two evils." His glance turned to the snarling, flashing turbulence fast approaching. "Though I'm not certain if there's much difference."

Silently, Bree's heart agreed as they kicked their mounts into a run toward the dubious protection of thunder, lightning and torrents of rain. The dust storm enveloped them first, and then great droplets of water began to pelt them. All at once, as if they'd passed through a veil, the world turned to water, roars of thunder and flashes of blinding light. The scent of ozone hung in the air.

The lesser of two evils? Perhaps facing bullets would have been wiser.

Bree's head whirled under an assault of sensations. Lances of wind-driven water stung her skin, and her drenched clothing hung heavy on her body. She could no longer make out her companions through the sheets of water that clouded her vision in the gloom. Teton's heaving body beneath her became as slippery as a greased pole.

She clung desperately to his sides with her legs and a convulsive, two-handed grip on his mane.

Then he stumbled and all contact was lost. She flew through the air and landed awkwardly in slimy muck. Pain speared through her left shoulder that had taken the brunt of the impact. For long moments, Bree lay on her side, fighting for breath. At last, she forced herself to sit up and then to stand, trembling in the deluge that had cooled the temperature by at least twenty degrees. If she didn't drown, hypothermia was a possibility.

Blinking against veils of water and choking in attempts to breathe, she hunted for a glimpse of her companions, either man or animal. Nothing and no one. She stood alone in the storm. A powerful gust of wind staggered her, and she slipped and fell to her knees in rising muck. Agony sliced through her injured shoulder.

She might not make it out of this storm. Thunder cracked and lightning ripped the air all around. One such strike could easily hit her, and that would be it.

However, even if she did survive to see the sun again, only one question would remain. What if the bad guys found her first?

Leaning low over Rojo's neck, Cam clung to his horse while his head turned this way and that.

"Bree!" The cry barely left his throat, swallowed in a gargle of airborne water.

The torrent and tumult isolated him as if he and his mount remained solely existent on the planet. The eerie sensation chilled him more than the abrupt drop in temperature. Shivers cascaded through his body, which Rojo's quivering hide seemed to echo.

He would have to trust God to bring him and Bree together again after the storm passed. And it *would* pass. Cam forced his overwhelmed senses to focus on that truth. He urged Rojo to slog ahead through the deepening muck on the ground. Their pace necessarily slowed to a near crawl. His stallion's breathing came in grunts as the animal fought to draw air out of the saturated atmosphere. This aboveground situation came as scarily close to swimming under water as the real thing.

Time inched forward, conditions worsened, and Rojo stopped still, head hanging, chest heaving. Cam clung to the stallion's back as if his life depended upon remaining mounted, which was not far from the truth with the level of water swirling around them up to Rojo's knees. They must be standing in a dip in the terrain for the runoff to be this deep.

Where was Bree? Was she all right? *Please, God, help her.*

He took a breath, and no water invaded his

nostrils. Was the rain's intensity receding? Cam lifted his head slightly. Needles of wetness pelted his face, but the dense darkness of the storm appeared paler. He could make out bushes and trees around him. His heart lightened.

Then, as if to mock his resurgence of hope, a deep boom shook the earth, simultaneous with a brilliant flash. Cam's eyes slammed shut against the searing light. An electrical charge stood his hair on end, and Rojo surged forward, nearly unseating him. Had his grip on the horse's mane not been all but frozen in place, he would have been thrown. As it was, he slipped from side to side on the animal's slick back.

All thoughts of maintaining possession of his rifle in the crook of his arm or his saddlebags across his lap were forgotten. What happened to those items, he had no idea. They were lost to him as horse and rider plunged across the landscape in frantic leaps and splashes.

Then, as Rojo's heaving lessened, the light strengthened and the storm's tumult noticeably abated. The stallion plodded forward, movements now slow and weary. Cam sat up fully on the animal's back and looked around him.

The plain now flowed with a film of water, in places cutting into the earth, perhaps marking future ravines and washes. The sky still dripped moisture, but in plinks and plops here and there, not breath-stealing torrents. Twilight yet gripped the air through dense cloud cover, but the sun's rays were attempting to peak through. Tempest had given way to a steady breeze that promised to dry the ground...eventually.

Cam didn't recognize his location. Nor did he spy another person, or animal, or any of his lost property. He could remain there and hope that Bree caught up to him. She'd been behind him. Or he could go looking for her. But where? In the storm, she could easily have become disoriented as to direction and ended up anywhere. She could even be trapped, wandering in circles, somewhere in the maelstrom proceeding across the plain in his wake.

Taking no action when action was possible went against his nature, so Cam seized the only alternative that offered the slightest possibility of success. He turned Rojo around and moved toward the receding storm, not fast enough to catch up to it, but with a steady pace that might bring him into contact with someone emerging from its grip.

Thankfully, there was no sign of the helicopter overhead. The bird had no doubt been forced to flee before the violent storm. However, the cartel *sicarios*' urgent orders to eliminate Bree might have forced a foolish decision to carry on. In that case, Cam didn't give the chopper much chance of having remained aloft. He might possibly come across the wreckage, but hopefully, he wouldn't. Not so much because he cared if the cartel minions were hurt but because he didn't want to take time out of his search for Bree to deal with survivors. Cold-hearted? Maybe. But he knew his priorities.

Movement caught his eye, and he squinted to make out a living figure emerging from the storm about a football field's distance from him. Teton. The gelding was limping and riderless. Cam's heart filled his throat. Bree had been thrown and could be hurt...or worse.

No. He couldn't allow himself to think that way. Bree was strong and resourceful. She had to be alive...somewhere. But she was alone and on foot, possibly injured, and almost certainly needed his help.

Cam called to the gelding, and the animal turned toward him and Rojo, increasing its pace with a welcoming whicker. Not severely lame after all.

"Where's your rider, boy?" he asked the gelding as they approached each other. Not that he expected an answer or even, as might happen with a dog, for the horse to turn and lead them in search of its mistress.

A whinny came from another direction and Cam looked around to find the mud-stained mare trotting to them, seemingly the least worse for wear out of them all.

"Good girl," Cam told the mare as she drew near. "Now, the gang's all here except for an all-important one. Let's find her."

The storm had drawn significantly away from their little grouping and appeared to be dissipating in strength and size. Cam urged Rojo to lead out in the tempest's wake. Calm now covered the land, the clouds had broken up, and the sun's rays were beginning to warm Cam's shoulders. His shivers lessened.

Gaze straining this way and that, Cam prayed under his breath. The longer they went without finding Bree, the greater the turmoil grew inside him—almost mimicking the intensity of the thunderstorm. Where was she? What could have happened? Visions of her trudging through the storm's darkness and tumbling into a wash filled with roiling water attacked his imagination. He worked hard at shoving the unproductive fears away, but the longer they went without locating her, the more likely such a scenario became.

There!

Cam rushed Rojo in the direction of an unnatural lump huddled among flattened grasses. His shoulders slumped as he made out the remains of a modest-size tent sitting near a swamped fire ring. Then a crawling sensation went through him. People had been camping out here recently. The tent's canvas wasn't nearly so weathered and tattered that the small shelter had been abandoned in this spot for any length of time.

Sicarios on the hunt for Bree? Quite possibly. And where were the campers, whoever they might be? They clearly weren't anywhere in the vicinity of this site. Had they fled from the storm on horseback or perhaps on an ATV? There was no way to tell. Any telltale tracks had been thoroughly washed away.

Cam left the site and continued with his quest, but more cautiously than ever. If the campers had been cartel hitters, they could still be out there, and they were likely to be armed, while the storm had stripped him of his rifle and the pack that contained his handgun. If the wrong people discovered him, he was absolutely vulnerable.

Rojo stepped carefully down a hillock into a small dip in the landscape where a temporary river ran with a swift but shallow current. On the far side of the water's flow, a set of smallish bootprints led to the edge of the rivulet, which must have been considerably higher only minutes ago, and then the tracks turned and led away from running water.

Cam's heart leaped. Those had to be Bree's tracks. She'd turned aside from crossing on foot and gone in search of easier passage. His eyes swept the area but spotted no movement. Disappointing, but at least he was traveling on the right trajectory. Cam urged Rojo across the water and began following the traces the wanderer's passage had left.

He wanted to call out for her but held himself back. If bad guys were out there, he couldn't afford to draw their attention.

Cam turned and checked what might be behind him. The other two horses had fallen back as they stopped now and then to graze. They'd be all right. He could return for them, but he couldn't wait. He urged Rojo onward.

Many fruitless minutes later, the stallion topped a rise and a flat vista spread before him. Across it, a small figure staggered along. *Bree.* Her name whispered gratefully through him.

Then movement drew Cam's attention below and to the left of him along the slight ridge he'd climbed. Barbed wire wrung his guts. A man stood behind a juniper bush, lifting a rifle to his shoulder with a bead on Bree.

Cam could shout and warn her, but how would that help when she had no cover? He could race toward the gunman, but he'd surely arrive too late to stop the man from taking his shot. There was only one thing he could do. And that was both.

Bellowing Bree's name, Cam clapped boots to Rojo's sides and charged the cartel hitman—knowledge of the futility of his actions nipping at his heels.

THIRTEEN

At the urgent shout of her name from a familiar voice, Bree whipped around. A bullet sizzled past her ear, accompanied by the sharp report of a rifle. Automatically, she crouched and raced away from the danger in a random zigzag designed to make herself a more difficult target. But if the gunman was as nearby as the sound of the shot would suggest, her evasive maneuvers may be worthless.

Masculine shouts from the hillside behind her drew her head around. Distracted, she stumbled over some small obstacle on the ground and fell to her knees in the muck. Pain lashed through her and she ground her teeth together. Even such a soft landing jarred her injured shoulder. The joint was probably dislocated. Not a fatal injury but debilitating when she needed to be swift and agile.

Come on! Get up, woman!

Bree struggled to her feet even as another bullet zipped past, preceding a rifle report by a split second. Groaning, she slogged onward. Her bootfalls splashed water in all directions, further drenching her sopped clothing. The thunder of her pulse in her ears muted other sounds. Any moment now, a bullet would end her senses and sever all connection to this world.

Then Cam's voice again, shouting her name, cut through the fog of fatalism. Bree slowed and turned. Atop the hillock, he stood tall, holding a rifle on a man who crouched on his knees with his hands raised. Cam had disarmed the *sicario* and stopped the attack.

Bree inhaled a sharp breath. Her legs went wobbly and she almost fell again. *Thank you, Cam. No, thank You, God. You sent Cam here in time.* Her thoughts drew up short at the unaccustomed release of prayer. Cam's testimony had deeply impacted her.

By an act of will, battling exhaustion all the way, she trod up the hill to them.

"I am so thankful to see you." She stopped several yards short of the prisoner with his captor.

The disheveled, dark-haired Hispanic male kneeling in the mud was short and wiry. His black eyes gleamed at her like cold pebbles. "You cannot escape us forever, *chica*." His tone dripped venom.

"You have not done well so far." Cam snorted. "I'm sure Señor Espinoza is pleased."

The *sicario*'s face reddened and his mouth opened.

"Oh, hush!" Bree snapped. "I'm tired of threats from your ilk. When we want you to speak, we'll ask you something. And, believe me, the rangers will have lots of questions for you."

The man's lips pulled back in a toothy sneer, but he remained quiet.

Cam nodded toward her. "We need to get to the nearest civilization so we can call your headquarters for an aerial pickup. The time for running and hiding has passed."

"You lost your saddlebags and sat phone, too?"

"Yup. But I ran across Teton and the pack mare a little way back. They stopped to graze, so we should be able to pick them up relatively quickly."

Warmth flooded through Bree on the realization that her horse had survived. "How was Teton?"

"Probably sprained a front hock, so he's not rideable, but we can put you up on the mare. Our guest here—" he gestured toward the captured hitman "—can take shank's mare."

Bree chuckled at Cam's usage of the old vernacular for walking. "We'd best get going then. Lead on."

"You're injured." Cam's narrow-eyed gaze assessed her. "I can tell by the way you carry yourself. Your shoulder?"

She resisted the impulse to shrug—an agonizing prospect. "I'm going to need a doctor to put it back in the socket."

Cam growled wordlessly, then motioned with the end of the rifle for the *sicario* to get up and walk ahead of them. The man complied with exaggerated swagger and a scowling face. Bree took up the rear position, clutching her injured arm to herself with the opposite arm to minimize the painful motion of her shoulder. Check that. Rojo took up the rear position, responding to a cluck of the tongue from his master.

Bree's estimation of Cam as a horse trainer continued to elevate. When word got out of his skills, he'd be doing a brisk business. That was, if they could ever bring this horrible threat from the cartel to a close…and if they survived the process.

Several miles of plodding as the ground grew ever dryer beneath their feet brought their bedraggled party in sight of a pair of horses contentedly foraging in the grass. At their approach, Teton's head came up with a snort. The animal started to trot toward them but soon slowed to a limping walk. Bree groaned. Hopefully, Cam's assessment of a strained hock was the worst of the damage. She wasn't the only one who needed medical attention.

Teton reached her side and Bree wrapped her good arm around his neck and buried her nose in his mane. The gelding let out a soft whicker as the familiar horsey odor settled her frazzled nerves. The situation could be a lot worse. She or Cam or both of them could be dead. And yet, somehow—and she could only thank God's grace—all of them, human and animal, had survived everything that had been thrown at them.

"Let's get you up on the pack animal."

Cam's gentle voice near at hand drew Bree's head around. He stood nearby, his gaze and his rifle trained on their prisoner, though his words had been for her.

She let out a brief chuckle. "How are we going to go about that gymnastic feat? You can't take your attention off the cartel hitman, and I can't get aboard a horse on my own."

"I guess we'll improvise." He shrugged with a rueful grin. "I can spare an arm to lift you up if you can be in charge of swinging your leg over the mare's back."

Bree grimaced. "We'll make it work."

She'd continue walking under her own steam if she thought she could handle the distance, but weakness saturated her limbs. Getting astride a horse would take every ounce of energy that remained to her. If only they didn't also have a prisoner to guard, the maneuver wouldn't be so tricky. But they did, and she had to do her utmost not to distract Cam too much from guard duty. She didn't trust the gleam in the *sicario*'s eyes or his crafty expression.

Together, the little troupe of people and animals walked up to the pack mare, who gazed at them placidly, her jaws working a mouthful of sweet grass. Bree took up a position next to the animal, and Cam encircled her waist with one arm.

"Ready?" he asked.

Bree gripped the horse's thick, coarse mane in one fist and flexed her knees to assist Cam's efforts with a hop of her own. "Let's mount up."

Her feet left the ground and her stomach reached the level of the animal's broad back. She heaved herself forward, letting out an involuntary cry as her shoulder screamed in protest. Cam's head turned to her. The *sicario* let out a feral snarl. Bree's peripheral vision caught brisk movement as he charged them.

Cam whirled on the threat, his support leaving Bree. She landed hard with her stomach against the mare's spine. The breath left her in a *whoof* even as the rifle roared and a masculine voice howled in pain.

The horse hopped once then broke into a trot

across the prairie while Bree clung on like a sack of grain lying across the mare's back. Her own plight barely held Bree's attention as her mind clamored with a vital question.

Who had been shot, Cam or the hitman?

Standing over the wounded *sicario*, Cam shook with the effects of adrenaline. The tussle had been close, but when the rifle had gone off as they'd struggled for control of the weapon, the bullet had struck the cartel hitman in the meaty part of the thigh. The *sicario* lay groaning on the ground and clutching his leg. But by the moderate though steady blood flow, he had not been hit in the artery and was not rapidly bleeding out.

"Now, what are we going to do with you?" Cam's tone emerged as a husky growl. "You can't walk."

"Help me." The man gasped. "I'm going to die." His eyes were wild with panic.

"Not so tough now that it's you that's taken a bullet. Relax. You'll live if you follow my instructions."

The man stared up at him, blinking rapidly.

"Take off your belt," Cam instructed. "Then bind it tightly around your leg above the wound. That'll stop the bleeding. I don't have anything for first aid or to help the pain. Sorry."

Well, sort of sorry. Not very noble of him, but he didn't have much sympathy for a guy who made a business of going around killing and torturing other people in service of trafficking drugs. The bullet the man had taken was a direct consequence of exactly that sort of activity.

Grunting and moaning, the *sicario* went about following Cam's instructions while Cam searched the area with his eyes for what had become of Bree. The mare had been startled when the cartel killer had attacked, but Cam had had no time or attention to see which direction the mare had headed with her precious cargo. Pent-up air gusted from his lungs as he spotted the pack animal ambling in his direction with Bree sitting astride her back.

Soon the pair drew close enough for Cam to discern the deep pain lines bracketing Bree's mouth and the pallor of her face. It must have cost her a lot of agony to get fully upright on the mare and bring her under control, but Bree had been up to the task. Cam's chest filled with a tender emotion. Admiration, yes, but also something more that he wasn't yet ready to identify.

"You're not hurt, are you?" Bree's query came out in a thready voice, another indicator of deep pain.

"Not me, but this guy isn't doing so well." He nodded at the *sicario* huddled on the ground.

She let out a disgusted sound. "What are we going to do with him now?"

Cam sent her a wolfish grin. "Leave him for the buzzards and coyotes."

The hitman released a string of Spanish curses while Bree simply raised her eyebrows.

Cam shrugged. "He can't walk, and we don't have a mount for him. Therefore, here he stays until we can send someone back for him."

"Your logic is impeccable." Bree nodded. "Let's be on our way."

The hitman continued to curse them. Bree shot an icy look in his direction and commanded him to shut up in fluent and emphatic Spanish. The cartel tough guy complied.

Cam swallowed a grin as he got down on his haunches in front of the *sicario*. "You had better hope it is your people who find you." At the suggestion of this very real possibility, the anger faded from the man's face and his look grew warily hopeful. "If you are rescued by your compadres, be sure to tell Señor Espinoza that Everett Davison asks the favor of him that he forget this vendetta against Ranger Maguire in honor of his daughter's rescue from the Ortega cartel. The debt will then be fully paid."

The hitman's eyes grew big enough to show the whites all the way around. "*You* are Everett Davison?"

Cam gave a solemn nod and then rose to his feet. "*Adiós*. We will send law enforcement to collect you. If you are still here, they will take you in, and you will go to prison."

The *sicario* began spitting curses again as Cam mounted Rojo. He paid no attention, and neither did Bree as she fell in beside him, riding away from the wounded man. Silence reigned between them until they were well out of the cartel hitter's earshot.

Then Bree sidled closer to him. "You must think the *sicario*'s people will get to the wounded man first before US law enforcement. Why is that?"

Cam sent Bree a wolfish grin. "I didn't search him and relieve him of any communication device. He must have one. I'm sure he's using it as we speak."

"I should have learned by now that you always have a reason for whatever you do or don't do." Bree pursed her lips and her gaze turned introspective. "Do you think Alonzo Espinoza will entertain the idea of calling off the hit on me in gratitude toward you?"

Cam shook his head. "If I thought that, I would have approached Espinoza with the deal sooner. But, no, cartel heads have a skewed idea of honor, if they have any at all. As I told you, Alonzo figured I'd been repaid when he let me walk away alive from my refusal to let him traffic drugs across Davison land."

"Then your message left with the wounded *sicario* was the initial gambit to get the attention of both Alonzo Espinoza and Raul Ortega. You think word will get back to Ortega that you're alive?"

"I'm nearly certain of it. The two cartels spy on each other relentlessly."

"And that knowledge will spark your ploy to draw both drug kingpins into the US after us as vendetta targets and in hopes of personally eliminating each other."

"To be hoped, but it's an uncertain prospect. We'll need to sweeten the bait, so to speak."

"What did you have in mind?"

"I'll fill you in fully when we talk to your boss at ranger headquarters. You'll all need to hear the last episode of my family tragedy—the part where my father was killed in the cartel raid—for my plan to make full sense to you."

A rush of emotion threatened to overwhelm him at the mention of the horrible day of the shoot-out on the Davison family ranch. Iron willpower barely managed to contain the fury and grief he'd been processing since the event. Judging by the gentle look Bree laid upon him, his pain had probably bled through his voice and expression despite his best efforts.

Silence fell, save for the thud of hooves against rain-softened ground and the swish of wind in the grass. The fresh odors of nature after a cleansing rainstorm always lightened Cam's spirits, though it had been terrifying at the time to pass through the violent weather.

Next to him, Bree let out a soft moan and shifted on her horse's back. Cam's heart wrung. If he could take her pain on himself, he would. They needed to find help soon. He strained his eyes, scanning the horizon. There. A distant line of electrical power poles indicated the strong possibility of a road running parallel, and a road would inevitably lead to human habitation. By his estimate of their location, his ranch site and the Maguire ranch site were far away. A road offered a better opportunity to make human contact that would get them to a hospital or clinic.

He urged Rojo to move faster. Not a trot. That would hurt Bree too much as she matched his pace. A fast walk, though, would get them to the roadside soon.

Within a few minutes, they were climbing a gently ascending berm toward the pavement. They came to a stop inside the fence line near a gate fronting the road. In the distance, a vehicle began to take shape, rapidly approaching their location. Cam tensed, poised to wave down what appeared to be the ubiquitous pickup that nearly everyone had around here. Few rural residents drove anything so mundane as a car.

The truck—a white Ford—slowed as it neared their location. Cam narrowed his eyes to make out whether more than one person occupied the cab. Yes, at least two heads showed over the dash. And what was that object the passenger was waving around like a thing he meant to use?

A gun!

Cam's heart leaped into his throat as he raised his rifle.

FOURTEEN

Heart hopping around in her chest, Bree reached over with her good arm and pressed the muzzle of Cam's rifle downward. That was close. They were wound too tight. There had been enough gunfire. They didn't want to invite a needless battle.

"No threat. That's the Trent brothers. Local gun enthusiasts. Wave them down."

Cam shot her a wide-eyed look and obeyed, whipping his arm up in an exaggerated stop gesture. Bree held her breath. The vehicle was almost level with them. The occupants might not see them, or if they did, may not understand the need to pull over. After all, people around here waved at each other all the time.

The truck swept past them and Bree slumped, air gushing from her lungs. Ah, well, maybe the next vehicle would stop. No, wait. The pickup slowed, halted, and then began to back toward them, angling onto the gravel shoulder.

Cam shot a grin at her. "One ride to the hospital coming up."

He dismounted, and Bree allowed him to help her do the same. Her knees nearly buckled when her feet met the earth. Weakness washed over her with a fresh burst of pain.

Cam turned away and slapped the rumps of their mounts, sending them back onto the prairie. They should be safe enough until they could be found and retrieved. Then he opened the fence gate, and Bree allowed him to support her through it.

The truck stopped and a door clicked open. A hairy face peered out at them, only the brown eyes and broad nose visible between a prolific beard and thick mane that looked like it hadn't met a comb recently. Except for their insistence on owning a late-model pickup and their avid acquisition of all the latest firearms, Able and Arnie Trent lived a rustic life, mostly off the grid. But they were decent sorts, as showed by their readiness to stop on the highway for bedraggled strays along the roadside.

Arnie squinted at them. "You-all look like you've been dragged through a knothole backward."

Bree let out a weak chuckle as Cam drew her through the gate and onto the roadside.

"She's hurt," he said. "We need to get to a hospital as quickly as possible."

Able poked his head forward, staring at them past his brother's beefy body. The only difference between his facial appearance and Arnie's was a lighter shade of brown hair.

Able let out a low whistle and clucked his tongue. "We just came from Lubbock. Got this piece." He waved the large, black pistol that had sent Cam into defense mode. "But we can turn around and go back. No problem. Hop in."

"Thanks!" Cam opened the rear door of the club cab.

Bree attempted to raise her leg high enough to ascend into the cab but couldn't succeed. Cam's arms came around her and lifted her onto the seat. She managed to scoot over and let him inside, too. Cam ensured her seat belt was securely fastened while Arnie wasted no time in turning the truck around and whizzing toward the city. Bree slumped against the seat and faded in and out of awareness as the brothers' voices prattled on and on about their gun collection and the new hunting dog they were training.

In typical Texas mind-your-own-business fashion, their hosts didn't ask what had happened, probably assuming Bree had taken a tumble from her horse, which was the truth, but not all of it. Their mounts lacking saddles or bridles must have sparked curiosity in the brothers' minds, but they refrained from poking their noses into the matter. Bree silently thanked God for the small mercy. If Able and Arnie were not aware of the cartel's price on her head, she didn't want to be the one to inform them.

At long last and yet in a surprisingly short time, the Trent brothers pulled up outside the emergency entrance of the University Medical Center in Lubbock, Texas. As Cam helped Bree out of the truck, she made a mental note that Texas Rangers' Company C headquarters was also here in the city. A very good thing—if they could get to it without running afoul of cartel presence in the area.

She opened her mouth to discuss the issue with Cam, but he bellowed out a cry for medical staff to bring a wheelchair as he guided her sagging body toward the entrance. A flurry of activity followed.

An hour later, Bree rested on an emergency room bed, her shoulder thankfully whole and in place once more. The pain persisted but at a much lower level. Her arm was cradled in a sling, and she'd been instructed to keep the limb quiet for a few weeks to let the injury heal. Then she would need physical therapy to restore strength and mobility. The muscle relaxant she'd been given prior to the doctor manipulating the joint back into place had Bree's entire body lazing against the mattress in a semiliquid state.

Should she be concerned about her current vulnerable condition? Somehow, she couldn't bring herself to care. Where was Cam? He'd been taken away to another cubicle to have his burns treated.

The curtain around her cubicle twitched aside and the man she'd been wondering about stepped in, allowing the folds of cloth to join once more and give them an illusion of privacy. Even though people couldn't see them, voices carried quite clearly throughout the area. Cam still wore his ragged clothing, but white bandages showed through the holes in his shirt, and his color looked healthier.

He scanned her up and down. "How are you doing?"

"Better. I'm amazed at how much a dislocated shoulder hurt."

"I'm not. Been there, done that." He shrugged. "How about we take off out of here? We may have only a narrow window of time to reach the shelter of your headquarters before our presence in the city becomes known by enemy forces. I'd be surprised if they aren't watching area hospitals, since I'm sure they've discovered we survived their kamikaze drone. Especially if the *sicario* we left on the prairie has managed to make contact and update them about us."

Bree grimaced. "Movement requires energy, a commodity I'm a bit low on at the moment."

"Good thing this place has wheelchairs." He offered a slight grin. "I called for a rental car to be delivered out front. Should be here any minute."

Gritting her teeth, Bree forced herself to sit up and then turn with her lower legs and feet dangling off the side of the bed. "Get me to a phone first so I can let my captain know to have a welcoming committee ready to let us in and guard our backs while we make our grand entrance."

Cam shook his head. "Already done. I got one of these from the hospital gift shop." He waggled a burner cell phone. "We can keep in touch en route and let them know our ETA in real time."

"Excellent. While we're loading up, I can make a quick call to Dillon and let him know to round up our horses and treat Teton's injury."

"Again, done. He's extremely worried about you."

Bree stared up at him, eyes wide. "You think of everything."

He snorted. "I wish, but I have to leave that omniscience stuff to God."

Bree had no ready answer to that observation. Her head still balked at yielding her trust to God, but her heart was more than halfway there. She wasn't prepared to talk about such eternal matters with anyone. Yet.

Soon, they were whizzing down a city highway toward Company C HQ. The activity of getting from the treatment room to the vehicle had roused Bree from lethargy. Seated on the passenger side of the midsize sedan, she kept her head on a swivel in search of hostiles following them. Cam's eyes flicked continually from the rearview mirror to the side mirror, watching for the same.

Less than a mile from their destination, Cam's body jerked. Pulse rate ramping up, Bree turned her attention toward him.

"What is it?"

"We've grown a tail. Big, black SUV three vehicles back. I've seen it one too many times." He let out a derisive snicker. "The bad guys never seem to get creative with their style and color of pursuit cars. Boring!"

Bree hugged her injured arm close as Cam increased their speed, not recklessly fast, but flirting with the edge of safety. He would probably have taken their velocity into the stratosphere if they didn't have to exercise a modicum of care for the traffic around them.

"Take this next right turn," Bree told him, violating the GPS directions. "It's an obscure shortcut that should bring us around the back of the ranger building. We'll take the lesser-used entrance to the underground parking garage."

She activated the phone in her hand that Cam had handed her when they'd gotten into the car at the hospital. Her captain answered on the first ring, and she informed him of their proximity, their route, and the presence of a tail.

"Keep coming." Captain Gaines's tone was grim. "I'll have ranger vehicles close in around you and cut them off."

Bree smiled. Gaines was a good leader. He must have deployed ranger units to be ready and waiting on the streets as soon as he'd found out they were on their way. Now, she and Cam just had to traverse the final half mile without being shot.

She looked over her shoulder, and her stomach clenched. The way that SUV was bullying heedlessly through traffic and creeping up on their backside, they might have only seconds before their pursuers came close enough to open fire.

The rear window of the rental car shattered just as Cam whipped the vehicle around the final corner toward ranger headquarters. The report of the gun echoed between surrounding office buildings. A three-story, square, brick-and-stone edifice loomed ahead of them. Ranger Company

C HQ. Straight ahead, a set of steel-reinforced garage doors grew ever closer. Thus far, the sturdy portal remained closed, and another barrage of gunfire hammered behind them. Pings on the body of the car informed Cam the trunk had taken hits. He started to holler at Bree to get down, but she'd already done so while speaking urgently but quietly on the phone.

Suddenly, multiple siren whoops bombarded the air, originating from different directions. Ranger vehicles converged from side streets. The attack vehicle behind them began to slow down and fall back even as the garage doors in front of them started to rise. For the remaining nail-biting yards between them and safety, Cam held their vehicle's speed steady. Finally, the car plunged through the opening into the relative dimness of the secure parking garage.

He brought the rental to a stop at the bottom of an incline, and ranger personnel filled in behind them with impressive efficiency, guns drawn and aimed at the ever-narrowing opening onto the street as the doors rumbled shut with maddening slowness. At least, slow was the impression on Cam in the moment. He had no doubt that, in reality, the doors closed more quickly than average, given their use in a law enforcement building.

Cam opened his door and emerged from the

driver's seat. Mingled odors of vehicle exhaust, oil and cool concrete met his nostrils. Bree had already piled out of her side and was peppering ranger buddies with questions regarding the attack on the headquarters building yesterday. From what he overheard, their second-hand information that injuries had been minor was correct. Another item for which to give thanks.

The tall, lanky ranger who'd been introduced as Dan Halliday out at the helicopter crash site a little over two weeks ago strode up to Cam and stuck out his hand, just like he'd done at their first meeting. Cam shook with the man. Then the ranger turned away and began to move toward metal doors with a sign saying Elevator above them.

"Follow me. I'll take you to Captain Gaines. He's waiting upstairs."

Cam gazed around warily as Bree joined him, along with two other rangers, the stocky Mitch Horn among them. The man's gaze on Bree continued to betray more than collegial interest. As much as the yearning look raised Cam's hackles for a personal reason he wasn't yet ready to confront, his wariness possessed another source.

He was beyond certain that someone in this unit, perhaps someone who walked with them this very moment, was in the cartel's pocket. Actually, he hoped that was the case to bolster the likelihood of success for his plan to lure out the cartel kingpins, though he hated the idea for Bree's sake and the morale of her ranger company. Everybody got smattered with mud when a dirty law enforcement member was exposed. He'd experienced the ripple effect during his tenure with the DEA.

At last, the elevator delivered their little troupe to the third floor. They strode, almost in lockstep, into a busy bullpen full of desks and moving bodies, and faces staring into screens. Carpeting throughout the area kept the noise muted, though the racket was distinctly familiar to Cam from his earlier career.

At their appearance, silence washed in like a wave as attention was drawn and conversations and typing ceased. The hush continued as Dan led them into a spacious glassed-in corner office facing the bullpen. It had apparently taken some rifle fire through a window in the outer wall, which was now covered by a solid sheet of metal. The repairers had made do with slabs of Sheetrock to temporarily mend the missing interior panes.

They stepped into the office where Gaines stood behind a bullet-scarred wooden desk. Only Mitch, Dan, Bree and Cam entered the room. The other rangers peeled off to continue regular duties.

"We made it, Captain Gaines." Bree stopped in front of the desk. "Thank you for the assist."

"Good to see you're whole. Well, almost." The captain motioned to Bree's sling.

Then he turned his attention toward Cam, who met the man's assessing pale blue gaze with an evaluating look of his own. Bree thought a lot of her boss. Cam wanted to do the same, but caution held him back. Even the big cheese of an outfit could be compromised. At the same time, he respected Bree's character evaluations. She was the epitome of a skeptic and didn't give trust lightly. For the moment, Cam would give Gaines the benefit of the doubt.

The man nodded solemnly and held out his hand. Cam took it and found the grip firm but not aggressive. Signs of a confident person. Another tick in the positive column for the captain.

"Good to see you again, Cameron Wolfe. I keep hearing good reports of you from my people, including Bree, and she's hard to impress."

Despite any lingering misgivings, the words brought a grin to Cam's face. "I've noticed, sir."

"Thank you for staying by her side through this. Can we get you anything? Food, beverages, a change of clothes?" His grizzled eyebrows went up as those pale eyes glinted with understated humor at their disheveled appearance.

A chuckle escaped Cam. Yes, he was going to have to like this guy.

"All of the above, thank you," Bree answered for them.

Gaines jerked his square chin at Dan and Mitch. "Round up some food and clothing while Bree shows Cam to the locker rooms. Let them freshen up, hydrate and eat. Then we'll have a strategy summit right here." He nodded at Bree and Cam.

"Thank you, sir," Cam said. "Any word on the attackers in the SUV who chased us here? Were they apprehended?"

"Affirmative. We've got a pair of cartel members in custody, but they're low-level thugs, not seasoned *sicarios*. I doubt we'll get much useful intelligence out of them."

"Too bad, but congratulations on the arrest."

"Follow me." Bree motioned, and Cam exited the room behind her.

A reprieve was welcome from the revelations he must make to lay the case for his strategy to capture the cartel heads. And a hot shower, clean clothes, and a meal sounded beyond great. A long sleep was also on the list of necessities, but that would have to wait until after the difficult conversation with the captain.

As if Bree and Cam shared an unspoken agreement to take a break from heavy topics while they refreshed themselves, only conversation on mundane matters passed between them while they went down to the first level above the parking garage. She showed him the men's locker room and then went off toward the women's.

By the time Cam had enjoyed that hot shower he'd craved, a set of clothes had found their perch on a bench by the lockers. The pants and shirt fit him reasonably well, and the socks were one-size-fits-most. He tugged his boots onto his feet, feeling clean and as alert as he was going to get short of eight hours of uninterrupted sleep.

As he reaffixed his watch around his wrist, Dan showed up, and they joined Bree and Mitch in the hallway. Another ride on the elevator brought them to the second floor, where they were showed into a small conference room where paper sacks emitting savory scents awaited them.

"Want us to wait around here in case you need anything else?" Mitch's tone dripped hope.

Bree shook her head with a perfunctory smile. "I know my way back to the captain's office. Dealing with us must have set you guys back on your workday, so don't give us another thought."

Mitch's face fell, and Dan flickered a brief smirk behind his partner's back as he followed the man out the door. The shorter ranger wasn't fooling anybody about his interest in Bree. Except maybe Bree, who seemed oblivious. Cam suspected she was feigning ignorance to avoid the awkwardness of acknowledgment, but the time was fast approaching when the matter would need to be addressed head-on. Now was not that time.

Bree took a seat at the table. "I'm so hungry, I could inhale this meal, bag and all."

Consuming the thick deli sandwiches, chips and gourmet dill pickle between healthy swigs of water took little time. Again, Bree seemed disinclined to talk about the situation they were in.

Soon, they headed back upstairs and reentered Captain Grimes's office.

The man greeted them, remarked how much better they appeared, and motioned toward a pair of guest chairs. Cam settled into a seat, and Bree did the same with a wince and a tiny groan. The captain came around his desk and shut the door, then returned to perch in his desk chair, leaning forward.

"What can we do to end this?" His gaze rested on Bree. "If there's any other option, I don't want to lose a fine ranger to WITSEC. On the other hand, we can't have your life constantly in danger."

"The life of a ranger is inherently dangerous."

Gaines shook his head and wagged an admonishing finger. "Not like this."

Bree hung her head. "I know." She heaved a long breath. "Cam has an idea, but it's risky and doesn't come with guarantees."

"By all means, let's hear it." The captain laid his hands flat on the desktop and shifted his focus onto Cam.

The pale stare sliced into him like a laser beam and heat jolted through him. Moment of truth. The whole truth and nothing but the truth. He was about to break a vow he'd made to himself to never speak of those final intense moments of gun smoke, blood and fear when his father died and the woman he'd thought loved him had betrayed them both in a scramble for wealth and self-preservation. Cam's throat tightened as memories attacked. If only his ex-fiancée's betrayal and his father's death had been the worst events that day.

FIFTEEN

"My legal name is Cameron Wolfe, but my birth name is Everett Davison."

Bree resisted the urge to take Cam's hand as he began recounting his pain-filled history. She sensed her touch might be an unwelcome distraction. He seemed to have drawn in upon himself, and his voice was thin but as strong as a sheet of tungsten metal.

Gaines had the good sense to remain silent while Cam went through the parts of his story Bree had heard already. Her captain's only reaction was an occasional flinch or a repeat of the muted intake of breath that had greeted Cam's opening revelation about his identity. But then the saga moved into new territory and Bree sat gripping her chair with white-knuckled fingers.

"We thought we were safe. That the worst was over after the Ortega human-and-drug-trafficking ring had been shut down on our property and Alonzo Espinoza allowed me to walk away from his proposition to take over the smuggling route through our land. My father was now under a public cloud of suspicion regarding his possible involvement in the Ortega ring, but nothing could be proved. He did resign from his position as state senator and then came home from the capitol. He also brought my ex-fiancée with him, scheming anew to realize his political aspirations through me reconciling with his dream wife for me and assuming my 'rightful place—'" he bracketed the two words with air quotes "—in high society. The atmosphere in the house was naturally strained, because I *knew* my father was involved with the cartel, and I had no interest in renewing a relationship with my ex. Despite my rekindled love for ranching, I was seriously considering leaving the Leaning-D permanently when the enraged Ortega cartel struck our home site."

A sharp gasp left Bree's throat and her face heated as she clapped a hand over her mouth. It was one thing to have read the lurid accounts of the tragedy in the newspaper and listened to the sensational reports on television. But hearing the brutal fact stated from someone who'd been there, and in the overly flat tone and bald brevity that signified great emotion held in check, was quite another experience. Bree's heart wrung like it would spring from her chest, and her hand flew to his. His return grip around her fingers quickly became almost painful before his chest heaved and he gradually calmed. Cam released her and visibly shook himself, his eyes fixed resolutely on her captain.

Gaines cleared his throat. "You don't need to share details of the battle. We already know several ranch hands and your father were killed before sheriff's deputies and border patrol agents arrived to help. Go ahead and move on to how this event ties in with getting the price lifted from Brianna's head."

"Thank you. I don't believe I will offer graphic descriptions. No one needs those visuals in their head."

Bree bit her bottom lip. She heard what he wasn't saying—that *he* could not escape those visuals. He carried them with him on the inside. The level of horror that Cam had experienced and the faith-filled grace with which he managed the scars impressed her beyond words. If only she could claim she possessed a similar level of faith.

Cam shifted in his seat. "I do need to color in a few details of another sort far worse for me but that were never released to the public."

"Go on." The captain nodded, face pale as if dreading what might be revealed.

"I didn't find out until afterward, and I was

somehow still alive, that my ex-fiancée had initiated the attack on her signal right before she took shelter in the safe room of our house. When I released her from the safe room afterward, and she saw what had happened, she was hysterical and blurted everything out to me. But no one else heard her confession. Raul Ortega had made a deal with her. If she would pick the optimal time for them to overwhelm the ranch, they would spare her life and cut her in on the money made through a reestablished smuggling route across the property."

"What?" Bree shoved back in her chair. "How is it possible she would have any ownership or say over Leaning-D property? She wasn't married to you."

"Yes, she was…at least on paper."

Bree joined her captain in gaping at Cam.

He let out a harsh snicker. "She'd lied to my father and claimed to be carrying my child, which wasn't even possible. Gleefully expecting an heir who might prove more malleable than I was, my father forged a marriage certificate meant to prove she was my wife at the time of my death. Unbeknownst to him, she also fully expected my father to be killed during the attack, leaving only her in charge of the ranch as my grieving widow."

Bree's thoughts tumbled over themselves,

struggling to comprehend the implications of what he'd said.

"Your father was in on the scheme?" she finally blurted.

Cam nodded. "Only he didn't think he was supposed to die in the attack. I was."

Silence fell as if all oxygen had been sucked from the room and every inhabitant had been robbed of the ability to breathe.

Hot tears sprang from Bree's eyes and bathed her cheeks. After such a devastating betrayal, how had Cam found the will to go on, much less to establish a completely new life and continually show himself to be a genuinely decent and selfless human being? Most people would be mentally and emotionally wrecked and bitter to the nth degree.

Her own experience of betrayal from her ex-husband, minor in comparison to Cam's, had soured her outlook on people. She knew that it had. Why else had she never attempted another serious romantic relationship? She couldn't blame her inability to commit to another man on cynicism from negative experiences with the worst sort of people endemic to her job. No, she'd allowed the wounds of a failed relationship to fester and draw her away from God and from deep personal connections with people.

God, I repent of my bitterness. Help me to let

it all go, to forgive my ex, and to heal. I want to be the sort of woman with whom Cam might consider exploring a relationship.

There, she'd admitted it to herself and to God.

Cam's witness had fully broken through her defenses. Now, they simply needed to solve the little problem of the vendetta against her life.

Simple? Ha! Try mortally dangerous on every level. But she was not going to run. Stand and fight remained the only option to achieve a life worth living.

Cam studied the expression on Captain Gaines's face—a scrunch-browed cross between horror and puzzlement. Apparently, the man was as appalled as Bree over the things he'd shared, but no doubt still wondering how his tragic mess contributed to solving Bree's.

"Now, I'm getting to it." Cam leaned toward the captain seated on the opposite side of the desk. "I've always needed to hear corroboration of Tessa's awful tale about my father's betrayal from another source. I don't trust her to have been truthful about my father's involvement, though I don't fully disbelieve her either. I know the man's obsessions too well. However, I've never been able to get the satisfaction of confirmation from an independent source. Raul Ortega is the *only* other source, and I need to be looking him in the eye, reading his expression, when I have the conversation. He will believe my reason for contacting him for a face-to-face meeting."

Bree reached over and gripped his arm in a python squeeze. "You can't risk yourself like that. He'll come to kill you."

"Not if I offer him something he wants more than me." Cam met her stricken gaze.

She gasped. "Alonzo Espinoza."

"Bingo."

Bree sat up stiff. "That's right. We talked about it. I'm the bait for *him*."

"Wait, wait, wait." Gaines lifted his hands, palms outward. "You can't mean to lure both cartel heads to some place on US soil."

"Exactly."

Bree's voice melded with Cam's as they stared in unison at the shocked ranger captain.

The man scowled like thunder. "And just where, pray tell, will this fateful meeting happen?"

"I'm thinking back where it all began," Cam answered.

Bree canted her head at him. "Where we rangers had the shoot-out with the rustlers?"

"Farther back—a place Ortega and Espinoza will know about."

"The shack in the middle of nowhere on the

Leaning-D where you first rescued those trafficked girls." Bree nodded, her eyes lighting up with something like hope.

"Not happening." Gaines let out a snort. "New Mexico is outside ranger jurisdiction."

"Precisely the point." Cam met the man's ice-blue gaze. "Ortega will be supremely comfortable with the location because his cartel is familiar with every nook and cranny of the area. And Espinoza is less likely to think it's a trap because the location isn't on Texas soil, where Bree is headquartered. After I talk to Ortega, I'll speak with Espinoza and trade him the location of Ortega's meeting with me for canceling the contract on Bree's life. He'll jump at the chance to personally end his rival."

Bree frowned. "Sounds like a potential bloodbath. They'll both come with massive troops."

"I don't think so. They'll be traveling across a hostile border and will need to move as surreptitiously as possible. I estimate maybe a handful of bodyguards for each of them, and we—" he swept his finger around at the three of them "—will arrange for a specially selected, but highly trained group of law enforcement to be waiting for them."

"Hmm." The captain sat back in his chair, twiddling his fingers against his desktop as his gaze turned introspective.

Cam fell silent and Bree was wise enough to do the same.

At last, the man sat forward and stopped the rhythmic drumming of his fingertips. "I assume this skilled task force will need to be formed on the down-low with as few people as possible having any awareness of what's about to happen."

Cam nodded. "Correct. But I'm risking stepping on your toes with what I need to say next. I'm happy to be seen around ranger HQ associated with Bree. And I want it to get out that Bree and I are going into hiding at a certain location in New Mexico. The information will get back to Espinoza and confirm the message I'll give him on the phone, as well as the one I've already sent through to the cartel boss via one of his *sicarios* today. However, I don't want anyone but you, Captain Gaines, to know about the deeper plan to lure in both cartel leaders."

The captain's expression flattened. "Because one of my people is compromised?"

"Isn't it obvious?" Bree let out a hiss. "How else were those rustlers prepared when we attempted to take them into custody three weeks ago? They ambushed us, and people are dead, including my partner."

Unresolved grief leaked through her tone and Cam's heart tore. She'd have some healing to do once this mess was settled.

The captain sighed. "I don't disagree with you, and I plan to flush out the mole as soon as possible."

"Maybe during the process of this sting operation," Cam said, "the culprit will betray himself."

"Or herself," Bree inserted.

Cam shot her a sidelong glance.

"What?" She blinked back at him. "Dirty rotten cartel moles can be female, just like righteous rangers. I'm equal opportunity that way."

He chuckled and shook his head, then turned his attention to Gaines. "Who do you know that could capably and quietly make up this task force?"

The man grinned. "I've got a good friend who's an excellent sniper in the Marshals Service, and he may have a trusted buddy or two itching to take down mega-bad guys. Also, the New Mexico State Police director owes me a favor, and I know he's not in the cartel's pocket. He'll have some good people who will leap at this opportunity with both feet." Gaines chuckled and rubbed his hands together. "Actually, the NMSP director will probably figure I'm *doing* him a favor for letting him in on this gig. He'll likely invite me to ride along on the mission." If smug had a face, it was the ranger captain's in that moment.

Cam chuckled and Bree let out a little huff. They both knew how law enforcement folks thought. Getting in on the action was a bonus, probably one the captain hadn't experienced in a while.

Gaines shoved his desk phone toward Cam. "Make your calls."

Cam shoved the instrument back at him and pulled out his burner phone. "The calls need to originate from a regular but unregistered number, not the blank number designation of law enforcement. And I'm going to have to reach out first to clandestine contacts developed while I was in the DEA before I'll be granted a direct conversation with the cartels' head honchos."

"Got it." Gaines nodded. "Bree?"

She grinned. "I'll take him to my office for his calls, while you make yours, Cap."

"I've always liked how you think, Lieutenant Maguire." The man winked and grabbed his handset.

Bree rose and Cam followed her on a straight shot through the busy bullpen toward the closed door of an interior office at the other end of the room. It didn't appear to have taken any damage from the recent assault on ranger HQ. On the way, she greeted coworkers, both men and women, who seemed extra interested in their movements. Cam saw what she meant about the possibility of a female mole, but he couldn't help but suspect at least one of the pair of male of rangers they'd come into operational contact with during this messy affair.

Was Mitch's seeming romantic interest in Bree a cover for his dark intentions? Or maybe the scoundrel was lanky Dan with the laid-back personality? Which one?

Cam shook off the questions as Bree ushered him through a door marked with a plaque that read Lieutenant Brianna Maguire. He sat down, cupped his burner phone in his hand, and released a long breath. Everything rode on the success of the conversations he was about to have. So wound tight was he, that he jerked when Bree's hand gripped his shoulder from behind.

"Wha—"

"Shh. I'm going to pray."

Cam's jaw flopped open. Miss Independent was going to ask the Almighty for help? A smile formed on the inside of him, but he didn't let it out. Instead, he bowed his head.

"Dear God," she began, "I'm rusty at this talking-to-You business, and I'm sorry for that. My fault. I'd like to work on the issue, but I'll need time and opportunity to do so. If You'll just see fit to guide Cam to the right contacts and give him the right words to say to everyone, up to and including the cartel heads, I'd be grateful.

That's all I'll ask for right now, but I'm sure there'll be more requests to come. In Your Son's name. Amen."

Bree came around to the front of Cam, went to her desk, and flopped into her desk chair like she'd worn herself out. Then she grinned at him.

"Go for it, cowboy."

Cam grinned back, his heart suddenly a thousand pounds lighter. Whatever happened—and the outcome was far from certain—something great had happened today. Was this the start of a trend? He had to hope so, but he needed to remember the old warriors' maxim that plans were necessary things but rarely survived beyond first contact with the enemy. After that, anything could go wrong.

Fortifying himself with a deep breath, Cam's fingers began to tap the keypad of his cell.

SIXTEEN

The southwestern New Mexico Bootheel was like a different planet from the northwestern Texas Panhandle. Standing outside the smugglers' adobe shack on former Leaning-D property, now in the custody of the state, Bree scanned her surroundings. While the Llano Estacado was an unending vista of grassy plains sliced with hidden draws and arroyos, the terrain here was rugged, with many milestone upheavals of land and even mountains in the near distance. The climate was drier here, especially after the Llano's recent rainstorm, and a bit warmer, though with a hint of higher elevation chill in the breeze that cooled her skin under the merciless, nearly noon sun.

Bree looked up, and her gaze fastened on a hawk lazily whirling on the thermals, eyeing the ground for prey. She shivered, giving thanks she was too large for the raptor to hunt. But others were coming who considered her the mouse in their sights.

A crickety chirp from a nearby cuckoo cut off her morbid thoughts. Then the odor of broken sage preceded the crunch of footsteps on brittle weeds and drew her attention to a tall figure approaching from his scouting expedition around the property. If only she could enjoy exploring the unfamiliar landscape in the company of the man striding her way, but she was all too aware of the minutes ticking toward the time for the fateful rendezvous.

This was really going to happen. Tingles swept across her flesh. Both cartel leaders had taken the bait. They seemed to have believed Cam when he'd assured them that only he and Bree would be present at the rendezvous site. Of course, Cam hadn't been lying. It was only the two of them here in the cup of the small valley where the shack hunched, crumbling and brown. Her gaze scanned the ridged heights several football fields' distance away where Marshals Service snipers and Dillon, an unsung sharpshooter himself, held overwatch.

Cam stopped beside her, and Bree sent him a nod, not quite managing to smile. The pins and needles attacking her insides didn't allow a light gesture. Nor did Cam smile. In fact, his face seemed to be battling a frown, resulting in an eerily blank expression.

"What happened to her?" To break the heavy silence, Bree blurted out the question that had been plaguing her for a while.

Cam's brows lifted. "Who?"

"Tessa. She admitted to those horrible things. Is she in jail?"

"Not hardly." He let out a sound like a cross between a snarl and a grunt. "Like I said, I'm the only one she confessed to, and then just at the spur of the moment in a sudden fit of hysteria after the fact. With the issue being her word against mine, there was insufficient evidence to charge her with anything. I knew I needed to disappear—and fast—so I pretty much left her in my dust while I went off the grid until I could arrange a new identity. Happily, I knew a judge who facilitated my name change and then sealed the records. I assume Tessa slunk off to Los Angeles, where she always said she wanted to live. The place is a rich hunting ground for someone looking to cash in, literally, on her good looks and sophistication."

Bree's hands balled into fists. "That just makes me mad. The woman got off scot-free."

Cam chuckled softly, and his features relaxed. "No worries on that score. I'm fully convinced no one gets away with anything in this life.

They either repent and get it forgiven because of Christ, or if they don't repent and a natural, human consequence like prison never happens, they still have to answer for it before God. His justice is forever trustworthy and absolutely inevitable."

"Huh! I guess you're right."

Cam's body stiffened. "I think I'm right, also, that Ortega is almost here."

He pointed and Bree followed the direction of his finger toward a dust cloud wafting upward on the horizon. Yesterday, at the ranger headquarters, Cam had told the cartel leader a rendezvous time twenty minutes before the time he'd given Espinoza, so Ortega was certainly prompt, if not a bit early. Cam had also predicted to her and the law enforcement team that the man would travel overland because his people had long experience with the terrain. Espinoza, he judged, would arrive by air, and Bree wasn't going to doubt him.

"Time to take our places," Cam prompted.

Involuntarily, Bree ground her teeth together. Was she ready? No choice. This was happening. She whirled on her boot heels toward the shack.

"Wait!" Cam called.

Bree turned to him and he wrapped his solid arms around her. She leaned into his embrace and stared into his smoky eyes. A yearning in their depths snagged her breath away. But he only leaned down and kissed her cheek then released her and stepped away. A little wobbly on her feet from the warmth of his lips, even in so innocuous a touch, she sent him a nod and then marched to her post.

The adobe shack's interior clung to last night's desert chill and goose bumps formed on her arms beneath her long-sleeved shirt. Holding her eyes wide to force them to acclimate to the sudden dimness, she moved over to a glassless window aperture. She took the sling off her left arm and then picked up with her right hand the rifle she'd left propped against the wall beneath it. She was Cam's first line of defense if Ortega decided to renege on his word about renouncing his vendetta against Everett Daniels if Alonzo Espinoza were delivered into his hands.

What had Cam told her once? Cartel leaders weren't very skilled with honor? Well, they'd soon find out. Meanwhile, Cam stood out there unarmed and prepared to have a tough conversation with his arch nemesis.

Bree lowered herself to one knee and propped her left elbow on the chair she'd positioned for the purpose of supporting her weak arm as it helped her aim the rifle out the window. She was careful to let only the tip of the muzzle show out the window opening. That way, Ortega would have the hint that Cam had cover in place and yet not tip the balance toward aggression that might kick off a gunfight. If everything went perfectly, not a bullet would be fired. If things went radically south, then hot lead could pepper the air like a kicked hornet's nest. No one wanted that—probably not even the cartel members—because some of them were likely to get shot. Cam was at the most risk of all.

Bree's stomach clenched as a dirty-white, off-road vehicle that looked like a Jeep and a panel van had had a baby began to trundle down the dirt track into the valley. Cam stood solid as an oak. What must he be feeling? Was sweat breaking out on his skin like on hers? His face, in profile to her, showed no emotion.

The thick-wheeled van with roll bars came to a halt in a cloud of dust about twenty feet from the shack. The van's windows were too dark to see how many people were inside. No one moved, not Cam or anyone in the vehicle. Bree's heart pounded against her rib cage.

At last, the van's front passenger door creaked open on grit-clogged hinges. Half a moment later, the rear side door behind the driver slid back. Simultaneously, a pair of armed *sicarios* stepped out on either side of the vehicle. The men's hardened glares swept the area and they held their automatic rifles ready to deploy at split-second notice.

Bree's finger cupped the trigger of her weapon. Any further aggression on their part would invite a warm greeting from her.

Then the *sicario* by the rear door nodded to someone inside, and a man of average height and build stepped down onto the ground. Ortega, she presumed. The cartel boss wore shoes so shiny they glinted in the sunlight and a suit cut like it cost more than Bree's annual salary. Designer sunglasses perched on his nose, hiding his eyes, but something in the intensity of his look reached Bree and a chill coursed through her. Otherwise, his features appeared regular, unremarkable even, though his thick, graying hair betrayed a stylist's touch. Take away the display of wealth, however, and this man looked like nothing special. She'd walk by him on the street and not give him a second glance.

Flanked by his bodyguards, Ortega strode toward Cam. "Well, well, the disappearing Everett Davison has reappeared. I half thought I would be meeting a puff of smoke." The trio halted several yards from Cam.

"I'm real enough, Ortega, and so is my promise to deliver Espinoza. He should be here soon, but you will have plenty of time to prepare a suitable welcome for him. I hope to be long gone."

The cartel head let out a hearty chuckle. "You are your father's son, devious and ruthless."

Bree was close enough to note the jerk of a muscle across Cam's cheek. No doubt he hated being compared to his father.

"As I mentioned on the phone—" Cam shifted his stance, leaning slightly forward "—I have one question to ask you about the attack on our ranch, and I will need to you take off your glasses when I ask it."

"Very well." Ortega swept the sunglasses from his nose and into his left hand. "What do you want to know?"

Cam's Adam's apple bobbed as if his throat constricted. "Was my father in on the plot to ensure the demise of his son and snag a tragic and sympathy-grabbing headline? Certainly, facing down a cartel raid on his ranch headquarters would be proof enough to debunk the rumors and assure the public that the Davisons were not in collusion with the cartel, would it not? Voilà! Political career resurrected." His tone was paper-thin.

"That was two questions, but I will answer simply." The cartel boss sneered a nasty smile. "If losing you meant regaining his aspirations of political power, the price was not too high. You know Emeric—or rather, *knew* his deepest fears and his highest hopes. You embodied both of them. When you refused to fulfill his hopes, he couldn't allow you to continue existing as his deepest fear—a better man than him."

Cam visibly jerked with every crushing phrase, but Ortega only shrugged. "You should take his desire to snuff you out as a compliment."

"Excuse me if I don't." Cam's words emerged in a gruff snarl.

Bree's heart wrung like a sodden dishrag. His pain must be beyond imagination. Then she shoved emotion away as Ortega and his men stiffened, their attention drifting skyward. Was Espinoza approaching from the air, like Cam had predicted? He was early, too. If so, everyone standing there was a sitting duck.

Far from appearing alarmed, however, Ortega's face bloomed into a broad grin. "You never asked me why I attacked your ranch. *My* purpose was to kill every insolent one of you, but you survived...until now. Today, my purpose is the same, and will include my only rival. It is good that I have taken precautions." He turned slowly about, motioning toward the hills and ridges.

Bree's blood ran cold. Had Ortega's *sicarios* silently overwhelmed her brother and law enforcement personnel on overwatch? Did the enemy now surround them, lying in wait for the Espinoza contingent to join the slaughter? Were they all about to die?

As a shout and then a gunshot echoed from a ridge, chaos began to reign. Cam dropped to the ground and rolled away into the cover of a pile of dry but thick logs intended once upon a time for the shack's fireplace. He'd stored his rifle there. Theoretically, Bree and Cam could communicate through a side window adjacent to the log pile, but the gun thunder was too loud for a voice to carry. She was comforted as to Cam's well-being as a rifle spoke from that location. Bree went back to her own job.

Gun blasts filled the air and bullets flew, not just from the ridge but from the air above them. Bree couldn't see the helicopter, but she could hear it. More hitmen piled from the off-road van and poured lead skyward while the first two bundled their chief into the vehicle. Even as she joined the fight, winging one of the *sicarios* and knocking him off his feet, Bree deduced from the starred but not shattered windshield, and the impotent ping of bullet rounds against the van's body, that the vehicle must be armored.

Bullets began pouring her way, and she had to pull to the side of the window so the adobe brick would offer some shelter while she continued defending herself and, hopefully, Cam, too, since they were roughly in the same location. The new position didn't offer her the best view of the enemy positions and strained her injured arm, but she made do with what she could get, methodically driving the crooks back from her position.

Then she paused in firing, the odor of cordite from repeated rifle fire swirling around her. Had she heard right? Yes, the helicopter noise had grown exponentially greater. A grim smile creased her face. The New Mexico State Police choppers had ridden to the rescue. The battle wasn't over yet, but it soon would be.

About a hundred feet beyond the van, a helicopter whirled to a crash landing against the side of the valley. Had to be Espinoza's ride. The bird lacked law enforcement insignia. Several people tumbled out and fell to the ground.

A bullhorn from above commanded the remaining *sicarios* to drop their weapons and lie face-first on the ground. They obeyed without being told a second time.

Elation left Bree's mouth in a whoop that came out embarrassingly loud in the sudden silence. "We did it, Cam. It's over."

She paused to hear his answer. There was none.

On leaden feet, Bree staggered over to the window that looked out on the woodpile. Her heart stopped beating, and her body froze. No sound reached her ears but the shattering of her heart.

Cam slumped, facedown, over the wood stack, rifle clutched in his fists and his blood painting the logs a deep crimson.

EPILOGUE

Cam struggled awake to the rhythm of an annoying high-pitched beep. At least the sound was faint, but then again, teasing him from barely audible range was part of its annoying quality. Then came a rustle and the pleasant odor of fresh rain touched his nostrils. He knew that scent. A warm presence loomed over him and his eyes popped open.

Bree gasped, recoiled, and then fairly pounced on him, gripping his hands and leaning close over his bedside. Bedside? Yup, he was in bed, but not his own. Hospital? Check. Now he knew where he was.

Cam gazed up at Bree beaming down on him. When did she grow so beautiful? Dumb question. She had always been beautiful; he was just appreciating it more every time he saw her.

"What—"

"Shh. Save your questions." She placed a finger over his dry lips. "I've got to tell the others. They'll want to be here."

"But—"

She flitted out the door. "Hey, everyone. He's awake." Her excited voice carried to him as the door swished closed behind her.

Cam had barely started to feel bereft when Bree came back, followed in procession by her brother Dillon and her boss, Captain Gaines, both beaming like she was. He couldn't help but smile back.

"We got 'em, my boy!" Gaines's voice held a crow.

"Raul Ortega and Alonzo Espinoza are in custody?"

Bree must have noticed the hoarseness in his voice because she put a straw to his lips and he gratefully sucked in cool water.

"You're half right." The captain's expression sobered, but only slightly.

"Apparently, Ortega was mortally wounded by the time they got him back into that van." Bree gave him another drink. "He didn't make it."

Dillon stepped up beside his sister. "Espinoza didn't fare too well in the helicopter crash. He's likely to join his nephew in a permanent wheelchair. They can share an accessible prison cell."

Bree gripped Cam's hand again. It fit there, and he wasn't about to let it go any time soon.

"We almost lost you." She started blinking rapidly and he tried to sit up so he could pull her close, but pain lanced his side and he fell back. "Oh, no, you don't, buster." She pressed firmly on his shoulder. "It's bed rest for you for as long as the doctor says. You lost a lot of blood, plus your spleen."

Cam grunted. "How about the law enforcement personnel? Everyone okay?"

Gaines matched his grunt. "Bumps and bruises and a few minor bullet creases. Everyone will live to fight another day. And one of our captives, Espinoza's right-hand guy, has been talking our ears off since his boss is in custody, too, and he doesn't have to fear reprisals. I'm extremely disappointed to tell you that Mitch Horn was on the cartel's payroll." The man's face reddened in a stern expression, like he was equal parts offended and furious. "He and a rancher neighbor of the Double-Bar-M kept the cartel informed of law enforcement plans and cattle locations, respectively."

Cam frowned. "*I'm* the Double-Bar-M neighbor, and I assure you it wasn't me working with the rustlers."

"Our neighbor on the *other* side of us." Dillon chuckled. "It was him who burned our machine shed down."

"Sorry to hear about all that betrayal." Cam scrunched his brow, looking from Dillon to Gaines and back to Dillon again. "I was worried about you. That initial rifle blast and shout came from where you were holed up on overwatch."

The man shrugged. "That was me dealing with the two-legged rattlesnake from the Ortega cartel who tried to ambush me."

Bree scowled, clearly not a fan of the danger to her brother. "The would-be bushwhacker will be taking a vacation to Club Fed as soon as they discharge him from the hospital."

Cam chuckled at the reference to a federal penitentiary but cut the mirth short at a sharp protest from his side. Bree's hand was still in his and he gave it a squeeze. She started beaming down at him again. He could get lost in her eyes. How sappy was that? He barely noticed a pair of soft footfalls retreating from his bedside, overlaid by muffled masculine chuckles. The door wheezed open then shut and Cam was alone with Bree.

She cleared her throat. "You have a lot of healing to do."

"You, too."

"But—"

"You're carrying grief you need to work through."

She huffed a breath and nodded. "You're right. And you—I can't believe—I mean—"

"I'll heal, too. More than physically." She'd been referring to the confirmation from Ortega about his father's bad intentions. "You'll help me."

"We'll help each other."

"That's what people who love each other do." He studied her brightly blushing face. "I know I love you. You do love me, too, don't you?"

"Whatever gave you that idea?" The words were skeptical, but the tone was tender, and she smiled as she said them.

He smiled back. "You don't have to tell me with words. Kiss me if you do."

And she did.

* * * * *

If you liked this story from
Jill Elizabeth Nelson,
check out her previous
Love Inspired Suspense books,

Targeted for Elimination
Safeguarding the Baby
Hunted in Alaska
Unsolved Abduction
In Need of Protection

Available now from Love Inspired Suspense!

Find more great reads
at www.LoveInspired.com.

Dear Reader,

What a wild ride—literally for my characters! Thank you for riding alongside Bree and Cam as they faced overwhelming threats from not one but two bloodthirsty cartels. They needed the everlasting Rock to lift them up and shield them, just as we do every single day.

What do you do when life overwhelms you? Most of us have people in our lives who depend on us. But even if we are going through a season of feeling isolated, there are others around us observing how we handle the tough times. Scripture urges us to be an example to them of leaning into God's faithfulness and allowing Him to demonstrate His grace time and again.

I love hearing from my readers. You can contact me at www.Facebook.com/jillelizabethnelson.author/ or jnelson@jillelizabethnelson.com.

Blessings,
Jill

HARLEQUIN
Reader Service

Enjoyed your book?

Try the perfect subscription for Romance readers and get more great books like this delivered right to your door.

See why over 10+ million readers have tried Harlequin Reader Service.

Start with a Free Welcome Collection with free books and a gift—valued over $20.

Choose any series in print or ebook. See website for details and order today:

TryReaderService.com/subscriptions

RSBPA24R